Deadlier than Corona
The Unyielding Social Infections

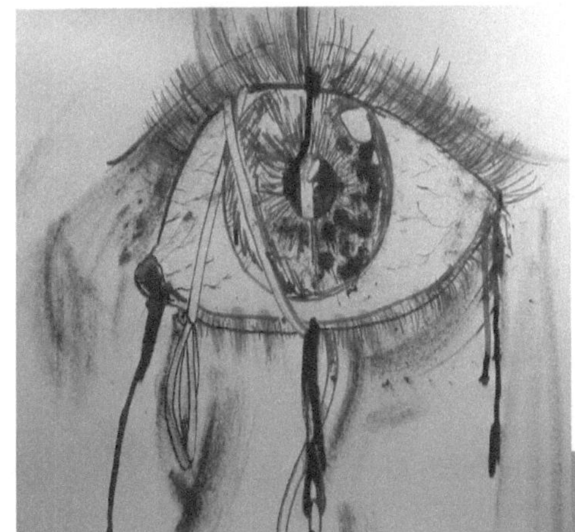

Satish Lala Kamble

kindle publication

ISBN-9798636325727

Forewords

Today the gigantic disaster, Corona is spreading across the globe by leaps and bounds and it, with all its strength, is trying to swallow the mankind on the earth. It has traumatized and terrorized the whole world. Hence, we all are at home out of the terror of getting infected by this endemic virus.

However, though this disaster is serious and enormous, it is temporary. Soon we all will get rid of the clench of this infection.

In true sense, there are stronger and more hazardous viruses than Corona; in compare to those viruses, corona is minor like a nib - dot. Some of the viruses had born with the birth of Hominid, the man in the prime stage and with the evolution of man they too kept on evolving and begetting other forms of viruses. Thus, they kept on spreading and infecting men and women so immensely that to stop and destroy the endemic of those microbes the God himself had to incarnate on the earth. However, the viruses were in their multiplication stage; they had become so powerful that even to God it was impossible to stop their spread in single birth. Therefore, he had to reincarnate time and again: once as Krishna to destroy the bugs like greed, injustice and treachery; thence as Rama to assassinate temptation, jealousy, excessive pride or ego, especially lower and mean approach to women. Similarly, when violence or brutality strangled mankind to deep sorrow, he had to take avatar of Bhagavan Buddha and Verdhaman Mahvir with the anti-dose so called 'peace' and 'love' to relive the mankind from violence.

Despite the God's endeavours, the viruses kept on spreading and corrupting man and the repercussions of those infections can be viewed in History books.

For ages and ages, we have been struggling hard to eradicate these viruses, but unfortunately we haven't yet succeeded to destroy these viruses.

In the present time, the bugs such as corruption, terrorism, selfishness, greed, hatred and eros   have hollowed many of the human-minds. The bug called addiction, especially of alcohol has destroyed a great deal of individuals and their families. Alcohol infected individuals and communities are far away from education and so from progress. They yet live extremely mean life. This addiction virus makes people commit crimes; so it is spur to crimes.

The bug, immodest concupiscence, is causing sexual harassment of women. It is begetting heinous crimes like sexual assaults.

 Thus, even in the time of lockdown and after the lockdown, there is a need to launch a campaign both individually as well as collectively, perhaps more powerfully, against the age old viruses which have occupied our minds, approaches, habits and thoughts. Remember they are deadlier than Corona.

So staying at home, along with hands keep washing your soft impurities and sanitizing your thoughts.

 Have a Happy Reading

Satish Kamble

It is true

Literature is the Mirror of Life.....

It is said 'Literature is the mirror of life'
because it brings out social issues, narrates
individual experiences, transforms cultural
and historical phenomena aesthetically and
portrays an unseen world.

Indeed, more than entertainment, it is a
social education.

WHAT MADE ME WRITE THIS BOOK ?

SCHOOL BOARD PREPARED BY STUDENT ON THE OCCASION OF 'NATIONAL GIRL CHILD DAY'

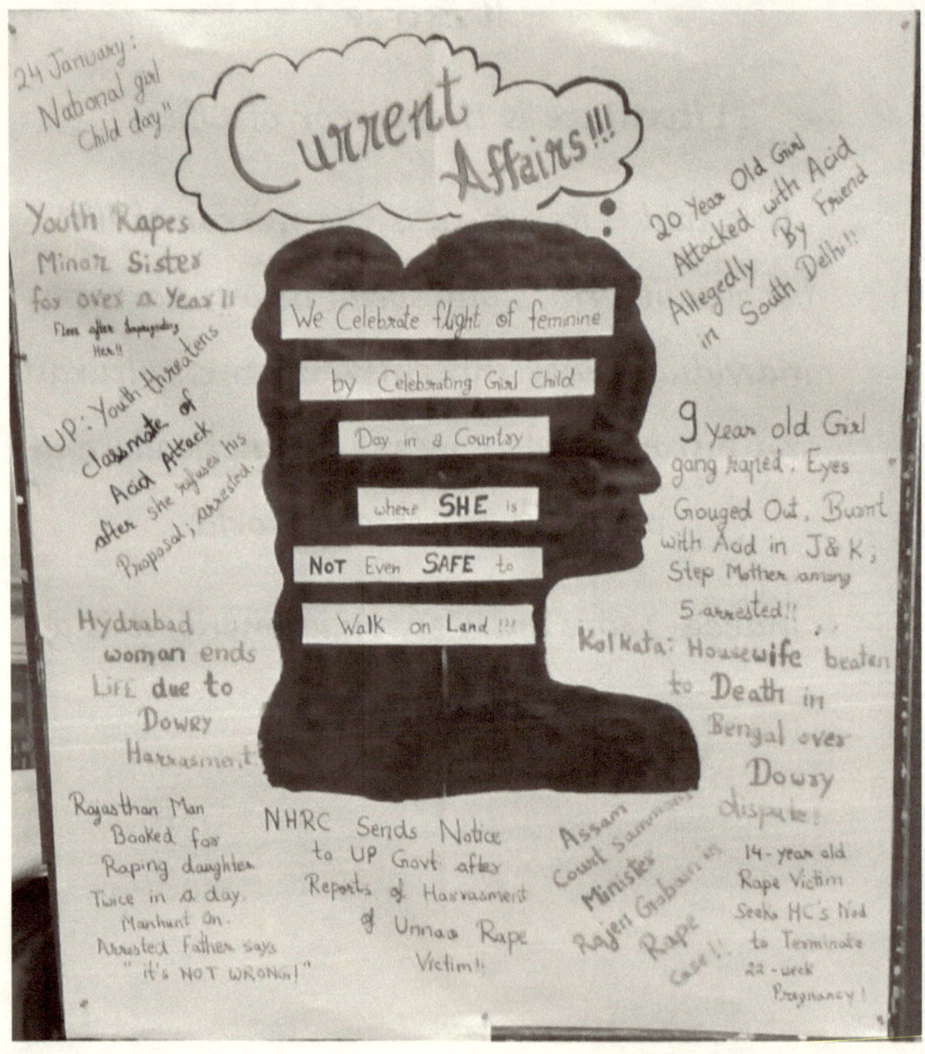

Writing a fairy story depicting an invented land with magical characters and adventurous events was a good

plan for me. But, the sight of the board, which was prepared by students of my school on the occasion of National Girl Child Day in the year 2018 refrained me from plunging into a fantasy cross-eying at the bitter reality. It triggered the writing persona in me; it stimulated me to depict the untold story of a woman I had heard of; and it also appealed me to bring forth the picture of a society that is indeed too dim if not dark; far away from the progress; having bland taste for education and deeply sunk in the slush of all social infections that I have mentioned in my Forewords and Preface.

DEDICATION

I bestow this book as a flowery tribute upon my loving and caring mother, Manda and my beloved brother, Nagnath who prematurely left for their heavenly abode leaving behind their unforgettable memories, immeasurable love and timeless words on the walls of time and on my mind.

As per my understanding, there are three types of people: 1. Educated by Degree, 2.Educated by thoughts and 3. The combination of both, which is rare. My father was illiterate by degree, but he was profoundly rational and creative by thoughts and sensitive by demeanour.

Before you start reading, I would request you to listen to a couple of pieces of this folk artist's self composed songs in his own voice, just as blessing songs: https://youtu.be/GPOS0gTY6Qk   https://youtu.be/Xv-TiwxNuK4

Special Dedications

I also specially dedicate this book to Vishvaratna Dr Babasaheb Ambedkar who opened the doors of education for all; struggled for bringing about equality in the society and preached the downtrodden to rise above all odds.

I am immensely indebted to my source of inspiration, my all time favourite author, Lokshahir Annabhau Sathe for sparkling my mind with his immortal writings and for inspiring me to create awareness in the society through writing as he did in the interest of socially challenged section of the society during his time.

ACKNOWLEDGEMENT

I am grateful to Ma'am Anita Edward for proofreading the manuscript painstakingly and giving it a cutting edge with her language expertise.

I would also like to express my gratitude to Mr Ravinder Rana who spared time from his busy schedule and rendered his valuable contribution in proofreading a considerable part of the book.

Last but before all comes Ms Namrata Divekar, my student who readily and willingly accepted the task of typing the manuscript. To your surprise and enough to make you utter 'impossible', she typed more than half of the text in her mobile. I am really thankful to her.

Preface

74 years have past since India got independence. Today it is triumphantly marching forward as one of the superpowers in the world. In technology, arts, infrastructure, sports, agriculture, education; I think almost in every aspect it is standing substantially neck to neck with other developed countries.

However, its oxymoronic socio-economic structure destines all its great climbs into falls. It explicitly reveals the atomistic progress. In any part of the country, one can easily find this juxtaposition of an affluent, educated and progressive society on the one hand and a poor, illiterate and backward slum on the other. Albeit it's a global problem, in India, it is thicker than any other developed country.

There are yet plenty of problems with which the country has been struggling. The social viruses such as corruption, women-safety, unemployment, poverty, and more importantly addiction to alcohol have glued to the nation like blood sucking leeches. To a large extent, these factors have barricaded the all-embracing progress of the nation.

Here, safety and security of women have always been an area of concern. Despite being ahead in every race of life, even today women feel unsafe to walk alone in an empty street at midnight. This is because of the fear of being assaulted, eveteased or being kidnapped.

Actually, women have always been an easy prey to lust, violence, ill-customs and the stereotypical approach of her counterpart. During the past few years, there has been a considerable change in their condition; however it is not the complete one. Yet the number of cases filed against_domestic violence, blackmailing, cyber-character defiling, women trafficking, abduction and acid-attacks is an alarming one. According to the crime data, 780 cases of sexual assaults have been reported in 2018 in India alone. Some of the analysts believe that the actual number could be double of the existing one if all women, without being vulnerable to their own or to their family honour or without having any apprehension of being abandoned by their husbands or parents, reported about the assaults to police.

Similarly, addiction to alcohol is another global infection. However, in India it is in its deadliest form, especially in slums. For ages it has been spoiling generations after generations. This addiction is actually a curse to the society. Many marriages result into divorces; every year, a large number of people die of liver-damage caused by intoxication. In true sense, it is a spur to crime. It is proved that under the influence of alcohol, even a decent and thoughtful individual can commit a reckless and unexpected deed.

In the year, 2018, in 46 percent of the crime cases, culprits were found intoxicated.

In my opinion, alcohol is the deadliest antisocial element: a potent threat to a family and to a society especially in slums.

This is also one of the reasons for developing reluctance towards education in youth.

At schools and colleges, it's good that there has been a lot of sensitization to adult education, gender unfairness, ragging, cybercrimes and many other such social, physical and psychological issues. However, we haven't yet given a serious thought to the equally perilous and life-destroying factor, the addiction to alcohol. Along with other educations, it is necessary to familiarize youths with its repercussions. It is important to educate them to say 'No to alcohol'.

Likewise, prima facie learners' dropout from education seems to be a negligible issue, but in reality it is not so. Today every Tom, Dick and Harry knows that education is an essential phenomenon if not for one's survival, but certainly for one to live a better life. Nevertheless, a large bulk of the learner-population quits education just at school level. And, the largest portion of this population is from slums.

According to the recent government data published by the Times of India on 2nd Jan, 2018, the annual dropout rate of learners at primary and secondary level has considerably hiked. It is 9.24 at the former level and 34.9 at the latter respectively. There are a number of reasons for this dropout; of those, addiction, lack of interest, lack of parents' attention and motivation to learn, people, practices and atmosphere around a child are the prominent ones.

For an emerging country like ours, such a hefty loss of young human resource is not an affordable one.

Apart from these, the social infections such as casteism and ignorance or superstition seem to be farfetched ideas in metropolitans, but unfortunately they yet very much exist in rural and semi urban areas. Because of the orthodox tendencies and the corrupt system, the communities under development are being deprived of the opportunities entitled to them. Consequently, there is not much change in their plight. They are progressing at the speed of a snail. A small percentage of the population is literate, they live in slums and most of the population earns its livelihood doing laborious and menial jobs like scavenging, sweeping, labouring, guarding and so on.

All these antisocial viruses are affecting India. Not only they are ruining innocent lives, but they are also corrupting and coaxing human beings to commit inhuman and disgusting deeds.

****

LAYER -1

It was a dark midnight. Beyond a dense forest, a little away from a human habitat, a dead body was in flames. The smell of roasting flesh had pervaded the ambience; having attracted to it, several hungry stray dogs in the vicinity had gathered there. Some of the patient dogs, hoping to have at least a little part of it sooner or later, had sat around the burning corpse while drooling saliva off their long hanging tongues. Minutes after minutes were dying but the hungry fire was becoming devastatingly wilder. Even after waiting for so long, they were not getting their turn. When they perceived that the fire was alone consuming their food rapidly, they started snarling and barking at the fire to stop it, but it was useless. With every splitting moment, each piece of flesh was turning into ashes in front of those hungry eyes and so those creatures, being restless, were producing kun..kun...kun commotions while watching it helplessly. However, in between, some rebellious dogs would boldly pace forward in an attempt to snatch a part of the body from the fire, but as soon as they would go closer, the fire would heat them and the poor beings would run back with surrendered yelping.

Eventually seeing the flames indulging in engulfing the body, once again those defeated hungry dogs barked furiously at the fire, and then turned their barking into a deep-throated wailing as though they were cursing the fire for keeping them hungry. This howling echoed in adjacent areas to *Samshan Bhoomi*, especially in Sathe Nagar and disturbed many sleeps.

In fact, it was a regular disturbance for the residents of this particular area. Since Samshan Bhoomi was the only crematory in the town, all the dead bodies of the town were cremated there.

Everyday there would be at least one corpse burning in it and mostly at night. Therefore, the dwellers of Sathe Nagar had got accustomed to hearing howling, screaming, crying and moaning, which are common affairs in a funeral ceremony.

Sometimes these screams would wake these people up in the morning and would begin their day; sometimes barking and howling of dogs would startle them awake at midnight to relax their scared children, and sometimes a rigorous mourning would lull them to sleep at the end of the day. Hence, for them the saddest event, death had become a humdrum-affair.

Most of the people in Sathe Nagar were from the socially challenged communities and economically underdeveloped. They would work like a yoked bull to fill their bellies. A bulk of the population, including women and children, would do toilsome, heavy and dusty jobs like excavation, construction, mining, porterage, farm working and working at brick furnaces. Some of the dwellers would work as scavengers, sweepers, cleaners, security guards, shoemakers, patrolmen etc. However, there were a few people who were not lesser than parasites; they were selling illicit wine and making money easily at the cost of depositing infinite curses of drunkard labourers' wives and children on their accounts. In reality, they were rotting lives of the people there; they were not feeding people with wine but they were injecting them with a dose of backwardness, poverty, helplessness and violence. It wouldn't be an epitome of exaggeration if someone called this area 'a kingdom of dirt.' In the locality, there was a wide-open plane to which all the people in the vicinity would visit every morning and evening. In addition to it, those dwellers would defecate there. That's why there was not much distance between the place of sitting and the place of eating.

In the rainy season, this open field would become a bog land of mud and human waste, and when it would rain heavily, all the excessive water spread over it, would flow towards Sathe Nagar. It would enter the houses and would fill house-yards and many pits and ditches in the area with it. This contaminated water would remain stagnant in those pits for many days.

Once mothers and fathers would go to work, the dupe children would play for hours and hours in that filthy water. Due to this water, this place had become a maternity home for mosquitoes and domestic flies. In this area if at all a biologist, studying different species of mosquitoes and flies, had undertaken his research, perhaps, he would have not only found all the species of mosquitoes existing in the different corners of the world, but he would also have discovered some new species of them.

This open field was called by a typical yokelish name 'haagandari'. In coutrysides, it is used for a wide piece of land on the outskirt where people would excrete openly. Some of the houses were so close to this field that the flies hanging around a human waste could sit on those people's food too. It might not have been an astonishing and ridiculous fact, had it not been a contemporary picture of the society i.e. of the 21 st century. Besides this field, there was an ancient common toilet built with black stones — nobody knew in which era it was built. It was so unmaintained that the WC containers would be brimmed with the waste with larvae like insects crawling into and around it. And, sometimes when wind blew north-south, every gust would carry a strong filthy smell of the toilet and would spread all over the residential place.

Now it was dawn. Smashan Bhoomi was silent. The dead body in the crematorium had turned into a heap of ash and the tired dogs were fast asleep around the crematorium.

Then, all of a sudden, a dog broke the silence with its intensively piercing bark at a human figure, which had stood just beside the ashes. However, the other dogs took no interest in joining the dog.

In fact, that Smashan Bhoomi was very mysterious. In the sunlight it would appear very pleasing and innocent due to the lush green lawn, fancy trees and bushes of round and large red and yellow roses around the crematorium, but as the sun sank below the horizon, it would look very horrified especially the dense forest around it; from a distant glance, the trees would look like hands with long nails erected from the earth. Many people had encountered with some supernatural being in the forest. So, once it was dark, nobody would dare to go around it except Badal.

 Badal was an unmarried old man. He would spend most of the time at Smashan Bhoomi and the remaining at Devya's Daaru Adda at Sathe Nagar. When he was barely eight years old, his mother and father died in a road accident. After his parents' sudden and premature death, his elder brothers just looked after themselves and deprived him of love and nourishment. Hence, leaving the house in his early childhood, he had taken shelter in Khandoba's temple at Sathe Nagar. Since then he had been living there independently.

Whenever someone would die, this man would become happy, because people's death would generate his livelihood.

Though the ash was warm, Badal collected it in a cloth, untied bamboos and hay from the pyre and marched towards the nearby lake carrying the knot of ash on his head and the bamboos and hay under his right arm. Soon he reached the lake.

On the shore, he went to his regular place, he slid his hand under a rock and took out a strainer, which is generally used to   sieve flour. He sat on the water's edge, hastily took some ash into the strainer, held it partially into the water for some time; and when the ash dissolved into the water, he held the strainer off the water, scanned the remains in the strainer minutely and threw it into the water peevishly murmuring some slangs. He kept on doing the same over and over again. After working for near about an hour or a quarter to an hour, he eventually found a blackish brown substance amidst the coarse particles of bones and coals in the strainer. This discovery brought a cheerful smile on his frowned sweaty face.

Now he was in a great hurry. He put his clothes off, went into a little deep water, plunged himself into the water thrice, swiftly came out, put the same dress on his wet body, hastily grabbed his things and went hot foot to Saraf market. The market was still asleep. He knocked at the door of a regular goldsmith; after sometime a voice broke from inside, 'Who is there?' ' Sahib, I am Badal. I have a gram of gold to sell,' replied Badal immediately and pleasingly. 'Come at 8 O'clock, that time only the shop will be open,' came this stringent instruction from behind the closed door. But Badal was restive; it was not possible for him to wait for such a long time. His lips had dried up and his fingers were badly shivering; he desperately needed to appease his agitated body. So, he pleaded, 'Maalak, I beg you for mercy! My child is seriously ill and it may die if he is not taken to hospital!' The next moment the door was opened. The goldsmith examined and measured the substance and gave Badal rupees 1900.

As soon as he received the money, he whizzed along towards Sathe Nagar and just in a few minutes he reached a house, which was made up of corrugated iron sheets. He entered the house and said teasingly, 'Hey you haramkhor Devya ! Today serve me as many glasses of wine as I wish to drink!' 'Why not Badal Seth, sit down and here is your first glass,' replied Devya dramatically. Badal took the glass greedily, dipped his two fingers into the wine and sprinkled few drops of it on the ground while chanting some prayer. His hand was still trembling. Then he looked at the other drunkards, Chandya and Sanjya and swallowed the wine in one gulp. Sanjya who had been gazing at him licked his own lips and spoke miserably, 'Badal, we too are very thirsty and so awfully restless!' But, Badal took no notice of his words. He simply kept on emptying glass after glass. Then Chandya convincingly said to Badal, Yesterday we did not get any job, but today we both are going for fishing with Narya, so surely we will have some earnings in our hands by the evening.' He then sighed and gave vent to his regret saying, 'But, you also know; until and unless Aakkabai [wine] falls into the belly, the day becomes an enemy – the soul boycotts the body!' Ultimately he came to the point. He joined his hands and begged saying, 'For God's sake, give us just a glass of wine, trust us, in the evening we will return yours!' So far Badal had consumed six glasses of wine and slowly the wine was taking over him. Now, he took the seventh glass, took a mouthful sip of wine and while looking at them, he gulped it and burst, 'Hey you Bhaadkhauo! If you are so thirsty, go and drink water from a gutter! Don't try to fool me. You loafers, I am not going to give you any alms!' He ruined their appeal; he did not give them wine, but he humiliated them with slangs. It was enough for them to become furious, however, although they fell into rage, they simply gazed at Badal crossly, but did or said nothing.

Now, wine had taken him over completely; his brain was out of service so he had no control over his words and his body. He was swaying back and forth involuntarily gibbering and saying whatever he felt to say. All of a sudden he declined on the ground and laid flat there. Devya slipped his hand in Badal's heap pocket, took all the money from it as his wine - bill and shouted, 'Hey Aayghalya Badalya! Leave now; vacate the place for other customers.' But, Badal was in such a condition, in which one can understand nothing. His eyes were half closed and in the trance of wine, he, like a jammed recorder, was mouthing, 'Naad nay karaych aapla! No challenge to Badal! I have so much money in my pocket that at once I can buy anyone in the world.' Suddenly, a thin stream of water ran from under him; he had urinated in his pants. On seeing it, Devya angrily stood up and kicked forcefully in Badal's stomach. It was so heavy kick that for a while Badal's eyes turned white; his breath got stuck in his heart; his waste erupted into his pants and blood along with many other things that he had eaten last night sprang out of his mouth. All these events happened in an alone moment. For few minutes Badal curled and coiled out of pains and then lay motionlessly while wailing agonizingly. There was a strong odour rising from him especially from the hideous pile of vomited things, which was lying beside him. In addition to it, a great swarm of flies was buzzing around him. 'Throw this king out at Haagandari and clean the floor if you want wine' hardly had Devya uttered these words when Sanjya and Kishya threw him out in a pile of garbage at haagandari.

In the evening, the wine addas would be fully crowded. Because at this time, people would return from their work with their wages and most of the men folk would first land on a wine adda. Before entering a wine adda, one would clearly remind himself that his hungry children were optimistically staring at his way for him to come and so he would determine to take only a glass of wine. But inside, after having a glass of wine his treacherous desire would urge him to take one more last glass and after every last glass, it would demand for one more last until the wine would take over him. Once alcohol mixed in his blood, he would forget everything. There, everyday at least a couple of quarrel would do occur for wine.

Now the sun was completely down the horizon, yet comrade Badal was lying on the heap of garbage. After doing a backbreaking work of loading trucks with heavy sacks of wheat and jowar, three chums, Nava, Somya and Kshiya, were now in the mood of having some recreation. On the way, they saw Badal in that ridiculous condition and they got an excuse to laugh; they laughed at him and also teased him saying, 'Badal ki shaan aur chaddi me ghaan!' In return they also received some dirtiest slangs from Badal.

These three pals reached their halt of recreation. It was Devya's daaru addaa. There, since their one more comrade, Raja had yet to come, they sat waiting for him.

All the four men were in the age-range between 30 and 36. They were married and had children too. Nava, Somya and Kshiya had no specific profession; whichever work they got, they would do for wages. However, Raja was a rickshaw driver by profession and he had four daughters and an old mother to look after, but this ruffian would work just for himself. He would indulge in consuming liquor, gambling, enjoying parties with friends and in spending his earning on prostitutes. His wife would do washing and cleaning work at some houses and would run her family.

Soon Raja reached there on his daily time and then their drink-programme started. Somya, while pouring wine into glasses, asked Nava, 'Today's done, but what about tomorrow? Any job?' 'Yes, there is one.' 'What?' 'Paving a house-floor and repairing its iron sheet-roof.' 'Where?' intervened Kishya. However, this time Nava gave priority to finishing the wine in his glass and began to gulp it in quick succession. Kishya, while drinking sip by sip, was looking at him and waiting for the reply. But, Raja had neither to do anything with the reply nor was interested in knowing it; he was busy in drinking. Now, Nava put the glass down, grunted contentedly and answered, 'At Hariya's home.' When Raja heard it, his eyes glowed and at once he told Nava that the next day he wanted to go with him to learn the paving work. On listening to it, three of them laughed at Raja. 'Want to learn paving work? Why? Aren't you getting passengers these days or what?' asked Nava ironically. But, before Raja could speak anything, Kishya teasingly said, 'He wants to do some part time job at night, don't you, Raja?' 'Whatever you say, but once I want to try my hand on it,' said Raja assertively.

While drinking they talked about Rakmaji's new affair and shared some funny videos in their mobiles. But slowly their conversation became absurd and their behaviour eccentric. In half lost consciousness singing, crying, laughing, dancing went on for sometimes and then Sanjya and Kishiya were flat on the ground; Raja went with unsteady steps while slanging to his wife all the way, and Nava's wife dragged him by his collar to home.

LAYER -4

With the rising sun, shadows began to detach themselves from the breast of darkness. In the mild sun-shower, Sathe Nagar bathed in a tender yellow light. Everywhere there was hustle-bustle and noise like a crowded market: as usual women were quarrelling at the common water taps; between the lines of houses children, with money and receptacles in their hands, were running helter-skelter after a baker. At most of the homes, women were busy in the morning routines like sweeping yards, washing clothes, utensils, fetching water and so on. In the background, folk songs on deities like Lakshimi Aie, Yedda Aie, Aambabaie etc were sounding in competitive volumes from those houses.

While, at haagandari, men folk were relieving themselves while basking their backs under the innocent sun. And while having this mirth, some of them were talking on mobiles; a few of them sitting in a group were discussing some last night's matter; some boys, sitting face to face, were sharing their love affairs; someone having head phones in his ears was enjoying music; someone was chatting and some boy was playing games on his mobile. Therefore, more than a place for abandoning waste, this piece of land had become an open forum for discussion, gossip and recreation.

Now men and women were hastening for going to earn their livelihood, but some loafers, wrapping themselves in blankets, were yet nicely lying in their beds either in the house-yards, beside roads or on Mitramandal katta[a common platform]. Raja was one of them.

Nava woke Raja up and asked to come at Vikas's house. Raja quickly took bath and ordered his wife to serve him brunch. No sooner did he finish his last word than she placed a plate before him. 'Where is the mutton curry?' asked Raja looking at the plate. 'Children ate' his wife replied softly. Her words kicked his anger; he picked up the plate and before she could utter a word or make a move, he flung the hot brinjal curry on her face and she screamed painfully.

On listening to her shriek, her children rushed into the house and seeing their mother's condition, the frightened children clung to her and began to cry and scream. The hot and pungent curry had gone into her eyes and nose, and now it was causing her great inflammation. Hence, she was agonizingly wailing, 'My face is burning! My eyes.. water...!' But, he, being absolutely unaffected by it, put on his clothes showering her with slangs and left. Then, some neighbors washed her face with cold water and applied some ointment on her face.

Vikas's house was a little isolated, perhaps, a half mile or less than that away from Sathe Nagar. Raja reached the house and stood at the door for a while.   He checked his hip pocket to see whether he had carried the required thing – it was in his pocket. Then, he peeped into the house but there was no one inside it, so he looked around the house and yet found no soul. Suddenly a sharp banging sound pierced his ears and startled him. He turned back and saw a tall and elegant woman in the bathroom, which was made up of jute-sacks. She was Vikas's wife, busy in washing clothes. Seeing her partially uncovered parts of her body from backside, his intention got strengthened. He swiftly drew a bottle of wine from his hip pocket and gulped it in a breath – for him it was simply a small dose to wet his appetite. Then he looked here and there. Having found no one around, a storm of lust whirled in him. His feet, being hunted by this force, voluntarily walked towards her. While he was moving, in the trance of lust and wine, his lips were murmuring something, his eyelids were quivering irregularly, his fingers were restlessly rubbing against each other and his steps were pacing forward closer and closer to her. Now, there was just a four or five feet distance between him and her. He was stepping slowly and stealthily like a leopard with his hands ready to grab her; in between a voice 'Ye Raja!' stopped him and made Jaya alert. He quickly looked in the direction of the voice, it was Nava's; he was approaching him. 'What are you doing here?' asked Jaya nastily while noisily arranging her sari. In a moment, he made himself neutral and with an innocent smiling face, he told her that he had come there with Nava for paving and repairing her house. Meanwhile, Nava reached there and asked him why he had delayed and without letting Raja to reply to his question, he told him that he had brought food for them and first they would have it and then they would start their work. Then, he turned towards Jaya and requested her to give them a couple of plates to have food. She hospitably asked them to sit inside the house while she hung clothes to dry. He nodded his head positively and both of them went into the house.

It was a 12 by 10 room, built in cement concrete. At the extreme corner on the left side of the door, a kerosene stove and all the kitchen material were kept and on its opposite wall, a shelf, full of steel plates, glasses, mugs, containers and dishes, was hung. A little ahead of it, exactly against the door a TV was installed on a wooden table under which a plastic can containing 15 liters of kerosene was kept. And, between the shelf and the TV an iron-cot was laid and above it there ran a cloth-line parallel to the wall; it was laden with old blankets, empty jute sacks of grains, some saris and children's wearing.

The men had sat on the floor. Nava was explaining Raja how to lay concrete on the floor, but as soon as she came, he broke off the talk and hastily opened the tiffin as if he was too hungry. She gave them plates, a jar of water and also served them two bowls of potato curry, some slices of an onion and two halves of a lemon. 'Please, do not hesitate to ask if you require something,' said she smilingly. 'Why not, after all, this is my brother's house!' Nava responded to her triumphantly. 'By the way, where has he gone today?' asked Raja anxiously. 'To Solapur, for selling toys in Gaddyachi Yatra [a gala of Lord Siddheshwar]' With little hesitation he again inquired her, 'When will he come back ?' She innocently said, 'As usual, after a week or a fortnight.' Listening to the last piece of information, Raja's eyes sparkled with some mysterious feelings and he broke 'Excellent! Simply excellent!' After that he looked at baffled Jaya and said, 'I have never tasted such a delicious potato curry in my whole life!' and then had one more sip of it. Meanwhile, Jaya's 12 years old son, Ravi and 10 years old twin daughters, Sonu and Monu rushed into the house shouting 'Yippee..! Today we have got a half day leave..!' They huddled around her and eagerly and competitively began to narrate an accident happened in their school. This unexpected arrival of the children disappointed Raja, it proved to be a barrier in his way. At that time, Somya came gasping and said, 'I have been looking for you men for the last half an hour and you kings are lunching here.' 'Yai you makadtondya (Mankey like faced person), tell us what the matter is,' Nava asked him coolly. 'Rakmaji has called you both at once to arrange a bull,' answered Somya. Raja, while washing his hand in the plate, teasingly asked him, 'Bull? A groom for your cow?' 'Yai Raja, don't waste time in cutting panchat jokes! You both have to arrange a bull for biryani; Devya has already gone to arrange a barrel of daaru, now let us go,' said Somya annoyingly and hastily. On listening to it Jaya surprisingly asked him, 'But, why?' Somya sat on the doorframe and told her pompously, 'It's a treat from Jhople Sahib to the people of Sathe Nagar! Vaini (sister-in-law), not to hesitate or forget to come in the evening to enjoy the treat.' She, while stressing on her memory, uttered 'Jhople Sahib?' and then said, 'I feel, I have overheard this name somewhere.' Being amazed at her ignorance Somya tapped on his forehead and said, 'Great! Vaini, don't you know Aamdar Sahib, MLA?' She tried to recall but she could not, so she smilingly nodded no. Nava smilingly told her, 'Vaini, for your kind information, that man had come to your door.' 'When?' she asked him surprisingly. 'Four years ago, asking for your vote – now remembered?' 'Yes, I remembered now, he had called me 'tai' and told me that his symbol was a crocodile and joining his hands he had insisted on me to press the button against it,' further she explained, 'after that flying encounter, I neither saw nor heard him, so like the saying, out of sight out of mind, I forgot him.' Now, Nava nodded his head in agreement with what she said and then showing confusion on his face raised a question, 'But, why this kindness in the blue moon today?' On this Somya sarcastically said, 'Hey Mr, later ask this question to Google maharaja, move now, Rakmaji Bhau is waiting for us.' But, Nava did not pay attention to Somya. For a while he thought over it and then while shaking his head he cheerfully said, 'Oh! Now I understood' 'Now what?' Somya annoyingly asked. 'No, your head is too small to understand it.' On this, children who had been listening to their conversation interestingly giggled, but as soon as their mother looked at them angrily, they muffled their mouths. Somya looked at the children and retorted Nava saying 'Mine is small but not empty like yours.' Nava teasingly laughed at this retort and asked, 'If yours is full of brain, tell why Jhople Sahib has given this treat.' In response to this question, Somya did not answer but counter-questioned him, 'First you tell me, can a fish be attracted towards a bare hook?' 'No, now answer my question.' This time in no time Somya replied saying 'He is feeding you because after some months there is going to be the election, and he wanted to book votes for it' and then while raising his eyebrow elatedly asked 'understood now?' But, Nava shook his head disagreeably and mischievously said 'Go and take a sleep, you need it' 'Ye, both of you stop your nonsense and let us go now!' shouted Raja irritatingly in between them and assuring Jaya that they would come back to do the work in a couple of hours, he left with them.

After they reached Mitra Mandal Katta, they came to know that that day it was Rakmajibhu's birthday and on behalf of Rakmaji, Jhople Sahib had given mutton and wine as a treat to the people there.

Rakmaji Chore was a Nagarsevak of that ward. He was running a daaru adda illegally in partnership with Devya. Besides, he was characterless, however he was rich and very close to the MLA, Jhople Sahib.

In the evening the birthday was to be celebrated and so Rakmaji's men were busy in their work. Some boys were decorating Mitra Mandal Katta with disco lights; some men were hanging a hoarding; some were arranging cooking material; a group was slaughtering a bull; someone was lighting an earthen stove; some women were winnowing rice and some were cutting tomatoes and onions. Thus, the preparation for the evening was in full swing.

In the evening Mitra Mandal Katta was captivating eyes with its colourful and dazzling lights, deafening DJ sounds were echoing in the vicinity and there was aroma of biryani in the air. The digital hoarding with the title 'May our promising leader, Rakmaji live a long life' was put on view pompously beside the road. In the hoarding, on the right side there was Jhople Sahib's a 10 feet tall portrait in a politician's favourite stepping forward pose and on the left side Rakmaji's. In the photo, he was in full white clothing with black glasses on his eyes, a broad golden shackle around his neck and a bangle around the wrist. There was a sword in the right hand pointing towards the sky and a mobile in his left hand held on his ear. Moreover, below these two dignitaries i.e. at the bottom of the hoarding, there were photos of loafers, vagabonds, hooligans and drunkards of the area as the birthday wishers and supporters.

Now, a great surge of people had gathered at Mitra Mandal Katta and so there was a great uproar. Soon a long and shining luxurious car, escorted with a police car, entered the area. No sooner did an announcer announced about Jhople Sahib's arrival than the hubbub in the crowd turned into a dead silence and everyone in the crowd curiously gazed at the way. In no time, the car halted at Mitra Mandal Katta (a stage for meetins); people especially children were left open-mouthed at the sight of the car. Rakmaji, along with a group of men, welcomed and escorted the MLA to Katta. After usual formalities and speeches, Rakmaji cut the birthday cake and the sky glowed and cracked with blasts after blasts of firework. People looked at the sky amazingly; the thrilled supporters and children once again formed uproar with their excited shouting, whistling, hauling and buzzing slogans.

After that, Jhople Sahib waved his hand and departed. Now, it was time to have banquet, and to enjoy it, women and children sat in rows on their allotted ground, in front of the katta, and men in the backside of the katta, some of them in rows and most of them in groups. Pairs of volunteers, carrying containers jointly in their hands between the rows, were serving food efficiently but lavishly. Apart from mutton biryani, there was an additional arrangement for men; the volunteers were serving them daaru to their satisfaction. Some of the men folk were greedily consuming glasses after glasses of daaru leaving the food in their plates.

Meanwhile, Rakmaji asked a man to play DJ music and provoked the men to dance and a group of men, being charged with the music, whizzed towards the sounds while shouting and whistling excitingly and began bopping and hopping wildly in rhythm before the sound boxes. Slowly more and more people joined the group and madly moved their limbs on the beats of thumping music. While dancing the people in the trance of wine were falling upon each other, stepping on the plates, shouting, laughing and crying too. Now, it was 12 in the midnight, yet the uproar was in full force. This force continued for another couple of hours with occasional breaks to chew tobacco or to recharge with a glass of daaru. Eventually, tired and over drunk men, one after another, dropped their bodies on the ground and stretched themselves wherever they had collapsed. Subsequently, people in better condition dispersed and then the throbbing music stopped, but in no time, it was replaced with snoring one. At that time, the ground appeared like a battlefield covered with the dead soldiers.

The next day, many of the men woke up late due to the late night party, hence they had to miss their wages that day. Raja woke up near about at 11 am. He hurriedly bathed, had brunch and slipping a dagger into the right hip pocket, he left the house.

When he reached Jaya's house, she was washing utensils in the yard of the house. Noticing his arrival, she gave a smile to him and said, 'Raja bhavji (brother in law), the sack of cement is behind the door.' In response, he nodded yes with no expression on his face and went inside the house. A pot of water, a sack of cement and a container for carrying the mixture had already been kept on the floor. In fact, Raja had neither any intention of learning that job nor any experience but still he prepared the mixture and started to fill the rifts between the tiles with it. He was waiting for an appropriate opportunity. He had kept a bottle of pure wine in his left hip pocket and a dagger in the right. Gullible Jaya was unaware of the ill intention of this demon who was right in her own house waiting for her to come in. She soon finished with her utensil washing, put the washed utensils in a container, picked it up and carried into the house. Perceiving her arrival, he pretended to be engrossed in his work. She placed the container at the feet of a shelf and started to store the utensils in the shelf. Raja was doing his work behind her. Since children had gone to school, except them there was no one in the house. Moreover, most of the men and women of the area had gone to earn their livelihood and those who were at homes had collapsed into undisturbed siesta, hence the locality looked deserted. In addition to it, her house was a little isolated. Then, Raja had a fleeting glance over her. She, backing towards him, was busy in her work.

The situation was absolutely in his favour. Now, his lusty eyes were scanning her from her heel to nape and gradually they were coaxing his sexual desire. In a way, serpents of lust were wriggling in his head and coiling around his conscience more and more tightly. Hence, his fingers were restlessly rubbing each other and teeth were grinding hysterically; he was breathing unusually; his face especially forehead was covered with infinite dots of sweat and his eyes had turned bloody. Being vertically shaken and hunted by his yearning, now he impatiently stood up and slowly and carefully stepped off towards her. But, in between, his tangled conscience alarmed him of the evil consequence and he stopped. He stood motionless for a while and then swiftly returned to his place.

Soon Jaya finished her work and went outside for washing clothes at her usual place in the yard. Sitting on the haunches before a huge flat stone, she began her work. While, being a pretending apprentice, now Raja faded away with the work and began cursing himself for having such a nonsense plan.

While she was busy in brushing, banging and squeezing the soaked clothes, she heard, 'Taye (sister), could you please give me a bhakari(bread of jowar) and some kalwan (curry) to eat!' She immediately turned around to see who he was and found Badal standing with a bumpy aluminum bowl in his hand. She did not like it ; she angrily taunted him, 'Lyi bhaari! Spend your earning lavishly on wine and beg us for food. You hail your tail away from my door, I have nothing for you.' In reaction to her words, Badal, pretending to look angry, stared at her with his enlarged eyes and said, 'You makadchhap! (monkey faced) I am like your father, don't try to teach me,' and then headed towards his destination singing 'ye duniya.. ye mhephil.. mere kaam ki nahi..' For a while, she stood stock-still seeing him going; she felt guilty of her words.

After that, she hung the washed clothes on the clothesline to dry and went inside the house. Raja had done considerable part of his work. She picked up the can of kerosene from under the TV base-stone, carried it to the corner where the stove was kept. She then hastily opened the cap of the stove's tank and bending over the stove, she began to fill kerosene in it. At that moment, seeing her partially naked chest, his lust once again began to crawl in him and with every passing moment, it became stronger and stronger. However, his conscience too became active and now a battle between 'do' and 'don't' swayed. His sexual desire was alluring him to do while his conscience was appealing him not to do. In this battle, victory was a deceptive phenomenon. For a moment, it would stand by the desire, the next it would be by the sense of his rectitude. Though in those few minutes victory played cat and dog with his conscience, eventually it won and succeeded in convincing Raja to give up his desire.

Now, he concentrated on his self-imposed work. Jaya did with her earlier work and began to pump the stove to light it up. In between, Raja, thinking to have some relief from the work, slipped his hand into his hip pocket, pulled out the wine-bottle, opened it hastily and swallowed half of the wine. Now Jaya was once again in his eyesight and the crawling serpent of eroticism in his head. Since wine had killed his fear, his conscience was now handicapped.

While she was busy in taking utensils required for cooking, being vulnerable to the trance of wine and yearning of sex, he stood up, pulled out the dagger from his left hip pocket and before she could understand anything, he embraced her tightly. Yet, she could not understand what was going on with her and who was behind her. She could just see a dagger in a muddy hand that was around her stomach, and another around her neck. However, when she realized the fact, she frantically tried to free herself from the clutch; she wildly scratched and bit his hands, but the swifter she moved the tighter he grabbed her. She abused, cried and pleaded too to leave her, but at any cost, he was not ready to leave her. She then threatened, 'Leave me or else I will shout and gather people!' On this he laughed smugly and slightly pressed the pointed end of the knife on her bare stomach saying in her ear seriously, 'Dear, dare not shout; otherwise this dagger will puncture your intestines! Understood?' This was enough to quieten and quiver an ordinary woman with a rabbit's heart. Being afraid of having stabbed to death, she stood helplessly sobbing and pleading repeatedly to leave her. However, he kept on doing all that he wanted to do. He pulled out the folds of her sari and one by one, he went on putting off all her wearings while the woman protesting poorly went on praying God to help her. But unfortunately, no miracle happened; no Krishna came to supply her with a chain of saris. She then ran and stood in a corner of the house shrinking her trembling naked body and yet sobbingly pleading him for having mercy upon her.

Now he was in no hurry, as he knew her weakness. He threw away the knife in a corner and roguishly said, 'Now shout, let people gather, let even a child of this area see you naked!' He then darted towards the cot and while sitting on it spoke casually, 'Shout.. Nothing will happen. People will come and beat me; at the max, they will put me behind bars, but no matter even there I will get a bottle; and for me even hell is heaven if I get wine there, and that is simply a jail and nothing.' She was crying painfully, nevertheless she was attentively listening to him and was secretly scanning the corner parallel to hers for the blade. Then, he reclined his back on the sidebar of the cot and stretching his legs continued, 'But I will tell loudly to the mob, to your in-laws, to your community and without fail to your husband that I have abused you. How about it?' His words sent a shudder through her. He took out the bottle; half of the wine was yet in it. He emptied it in a gulp and spoke in a wobbly but poetic manner, 'Do you know Ram, the God, Sita's husband who defeated the mighty Ravana for his wife, Sita?' However, she did not respond to him, so he shouted, 'Tell me yes or no!' To this, she startled and while sobbing she nodded yes. 'Now listen to me carefully. One day this God overheard someone saying 'Being enchanted by Sita's beauty, Ravana had abducted her and she was in Lanka for many days' and the next day this husband, Ram expelled his beloved wife, Sita.' Saying so he stood up, closed the door and sauntered towards her saying, 'And I am sure, your husband is simply a man, an ordinary husband, full of ego, anger, jealousy and possessiveness, isn't he?' His indirect threat and his approach moved her heart rigorously. Her nervousness stung her and her sobbing got stuck into her throat.

Now he was just before her. Pressing her one side on the corner, she profusely said 'no'. She then broke down and joining her hands implored, 'For God's sake have mercy upon me and my children! Please, don't spoil my happy conjugal life!' He laughed and said 'No not at all, just once satisfy me and forget it like a nightmare' and then he fastened his hands around her naked waist.

LAYER -8

The sun had completely downed. Badal was going to Smashan Bhoomi to check if there was something for him to arrange for his food and wine. Since morning he had got nothing in the ashes, he had been hungry and restless for wine. On his way, he found a couple of dead hens lying in a pile of garbage. This sight brought a smile to his face, but just then, he became conscious of the fact that they had died of bird flu. With this realization, his smiling face frowned. For a while, he pondered over something and then left towards his destination.

By the time he reached Smashan Bhoomi, darkness had spread its full-fledged wings over that place. He wandered around the crematorium poking and turning over things with a stick for half an hour, but all in vain. After that, he, with dropped shoulders, went to the public auditorium that stood facing the crematorium, approximately 70 or 75 feet away from it. This auditorium was made for the people in a funeral to sit and wait while the dead one is being cremated and burned.

Smashan Bhoomi was a large area stretched in near about 50 acres of land, out of that approximately 96 percent of the land, the forest alone had occupied. However, at the centre only on a patch of few acres of lush green lawn, there were a couple of crematoriums and the public hall surrounded by bushes of vivid flowers, fancy bushes, trees and hedges. That's why under the bright sun, this central part of Smashan Bhomi looked like a delectable panorama but at night there was an opposite story.

An hour had past, yet Badal, being all alone, detached from the rest of the world, had glued to the same place in that dark forest. Resting his chin on the embraced knees, he was aimlessly gazing through the darkness.   Suddenly, a faint deep-throated cry accompanied with an odd music struck his ears and he noisily stood up. He carefully listened to the sound and there came a bright smile on his face. 'Yes, a dead body is coming!' said he cheerfully.

 Soon the funeral procession arrived there. Now, the place was filled with wailing and crying of the dead one's near and dear ones. Since it was a night, those people performed the funeral ceremony at a fast pace, set the body on flames and   no sooner did they carry out the last ritual than the men folk insisted on everybody to leave the place.

Once the kith and kin left, once again silence restored there. The dead man in the arms of fire and Badal in his worries in the hall were now alone. However, without losing any time, Badal began his work; he untied three bamboos from the pyre on which the cadaver was carried, picked them up on his shoulders and directly went to Sathe Nagar to sell them. He sold them for Rs 50 to his regular customer and although he was hungry, he did not buy any food for him but straightway went to Devya's daaru aadda and bought two pouches of wine. He then again started his way to Smashan Bhoomi. While going he took those two dead hens from the garbage and marched towards his destination.

When he entered Smashan Bhoomi , his eyes dazzled with the glow of burning fire. The whole surrounding around the crematorium seemed bathed in the golden brightness. As only the lower logs had caught fire, the dead body was not yet much affected. He was rapaciously hungry so he thought that first he would roast the hens on the fire and only after eating them he would drink the wine. But, in the next minute, he changed his mind. He cut one of the wine-pouches with his teeth, wolfed it down. Then he felt that instead of searching gold in the ash in the morning, he would check the corpse right away.

It might be approximately a quarter to twelve; across the forest, Sathe Nagar was dead to the world. Badal then took a bamboo-stick and went to the burning dead body. He stood beside the pyre; the flames around the body were fluttering and flurrying with the puff of swishing air. The dead in the fire was looking horrible: the eyes in the skull were looking like burnt out brinjals; the flesh of nose and upper lip was completely burnt and so the teeth were bare – that gave it the look of a mischievous smile; off and on, the skull was emitting smoke off the ears and nose. Gradually, rest of the body–skin was melting and spreading the smell of burning flesh in the vicinity. Badal then initiated the examination of the corpse: with the stick, he poked the burnt fingers; pushed the chin up; moved the legs and even the skull, but unfortunately, he did not find any ornament. Eventually, with great difficulty, he slipped the other end of the stick between the upper and lower teeth of the skull to see if there was any gold in its mouth. Then, with a jerk, he pushed the upper jaw up, and as soon as the mouth opened, a gust of smoke sprang up out of the mouth. Flames were now furious; the time was odd; the place was horribly isolated and Badal was all alone. For checking the opened mouth, he went so close to it that his body received intolerable heat. He again and again poked the burnt out tongue but there was nothing in the mouth too. This checking assassinated his hope and precipitated him into a deep worry. For a minute, he stood motionless staring at the burning body. Suddenly, he felt something and gave the burning body a forceful wallop with the stick, and one after another, he kept on flogging it. In frustration, he kept on thrashing the body so madly that the skull, ribs, and other bones   cracked like eggshells. Finally, his body stooped supporting him. He felt increasingly exhausted and so he stopped. Now, he had no strength even to reach the public hall that was just a few yards away from the crematorium. However, somehow he managed to reach there.

Now, he felt extremely hungry and tired. He thought that he would first drink some wine to get relief from the tiredness and then he would roast the hens. Thinking so, he drank some wine and once the wine wet his throat, his wish kept on craving for one more sip after every last sip until the second pouch too was over. Once alcohol got mixed in his blood, his hunger vanished. He forgot his pains, sorrows and worries and almost for the next half an hour, he sat wailing, rebuking and slanging the burning corpse for not carrying any gold. Thereafter, he laid down and soon fell asleep.

Near about after two hours, wailing and barking of stray dogs woke Badal up. Now, he felt increasingly weak; his hunger had then reached the highest peak of unbearableness, nevertheless he stood up and with great difficulty went to the corner where he had kept the hens. But, to his surprise, there were no hens. He looked for them everywhere in the hall, but they were nowhere. His stomach was rigorously appealing him for filling it up with something but his exhausted body had no more strength to make any further movement. His eyes were fixed on the fire but the mind was occupied in recollecting where he had kept the hens. In the meantime, his eyesight shifted to something beside the crematorium. He suspiciously but minutely scanned it; there were some white loose feathers lying beside a dog, which had slept contentedly. Now, there was neither food nor gold in the ashes for tomorrow's food and not even daaru to bear his voracious hunger.

Badal, dragging his left leg , painfully walked into the hall and sat helplessly propping his back and head against a wall. His head was numb and his wet eyes were glowed with the flash of a flickering flame. Soon the last flame expired; the corpse turned into ashes; the flames into coal and Badal along with the whole Smashan Bhoomi submerged into darkness.

The front patch inside the door was illuminated by a torrent of sunlight. And, since it was a winter morning, Nava's wife, Neela, had kept her eight month old baby there for basking under the tender sun. The baby, playing with its own hands and legs, was cheerfully grunting in that winter warmth.

However, the baby's joyful vocals broke down its father's slumber. The father rose from his bed and ran towards the field with a pot of water in his hand. After returning, he hurriedly gargled his mouth, poured a few mugs of water on himself, somehow wiped his face with a towel, wrapped the same towel around his wet body and walked hotfoot into the house. He stood in front of the blurred mirror fixed on the door of an old iron-cupboard pretending to comb his hair. Then, he glanced at his wife from the corner of his eyes; she was busy in cooking. Taking its advantage, he softly opened the cupboard and took out a pouch of daaru which he had kept secretly last night. He swiftly cut its corner with his teeth and began to suck on it. In the meanwhile, Neela saw him and shouted, 'Gulp down! Gulp down some more packets, you son of bitch! Just the day has broken and...' She paused noticing that despite her shouting he was yet drinking. His advancement irritated her a lot but she calmed herself down and regretfully murmured, 'It's useless to talk to this useless man!' and resumed her work. Soon she wrapped her cooking up, put a big container of water on the stove to warm for her bath and then went outside for washing clothes to the bathroom made of some plastic sacks and hoarding sheets.

After consuming half of the pouch of daaru, Nava contentedly rumbled and mumbled, 'Now it's morning!' He then took a bowl from the shelf and a couple of chapattis from a basket and sat down beside the stove on which water was warming. After that, he poured the remaining daaru in the bowl; crushed the chapattis in it and devoured the thick soupy concoction with sucking noise. This alcoholic treat made him as drowsy as a rat-swallowed python. He hazily washed his hand in the bowl, however when he tried to get up, his legs trembled but somehow he balanced them and went wobbly to the other corner of the room to get ready for going to the work.

Now, the water on the stove was boiling. By the time he put on his clothes, he was completely under the influence of alcohol. He then laid down beside his child and began to tickle it to make it laugh. The more the baby laughed, the more he titillated it. He did it repeatedly. At last, the kid was almost choked with laughter and now it was desperately gasping for breathes, yet he was not ready to stop. Moreover, since Neela was busy in clothe-washing, there was no one in the house to stop him. At this time, only the boiling water was whispering mildly while the baby was mutely but frenziedly jostling and kicking in the air, perhaps, struggling for its life. In the meanwhile, "Bring the warm water here in Nahani" a high-pitched command of Neela from the bathroom stopped him. Thus, the baby sighed for the relief and laid down breathing deeply and heavily.

The water on the stove had been boiling furiously for a long time. Although he was drunk and in an unsteady condition, he stood up to execute the order. He went to the stove with unstable steps, bent over the container swaying back and forth and as soon as he gripped the hot top-edge of the container with bare hands, he jerked his hands back with a wail. He then took out his shirt and clenching on the hot edge with the shirt, somehow he picked the container up and woozily reached at the door. Suddenly, his hold on the container slackened and the container brimmed with the deadly hot water slipped off his hands and with that the baby gave out a shrill cry. Hearing this painful and piercing cry, Neela and even some neighbours ran into the house and saw; the baby was wet and vapours were arising up from her trembling body; it was severely burned. Seeing the child in that horrified condition, the mother screamed agonizingly and collapsed on the ground.

Immediately, the neighbours took the baby to a hospital. Sensing the baby's critical condition, the doctor straightaway admitted it into the ICU ward. The baby's mother was both agonized and angry; sitting on the stair of the hospital, she was crying painfully for her child and in between cursing her husband with the worst of slangs she had. Almost for an hour, she had been alternately mourning and cursing. While, Nava, sitting in a corner of the waiting room by sinking his head in between his hugged knees, was sobbing like a guilty schoolboy. He was now in a neutral state and so he was feeling the pains of his child caused by him. In the meantime, a nurse approached Neela and asked her to deposit fifteen thousand rupees. However, at present she had only three hundred rupees that she had secretly saved from the household expenditure. But, although it was a hefty amount, anyhow she had to arrange it to save her child. But, arranging that big amount in the short span of time was almost impossible thing to her. Therefore, she pleaded the nurse to give a day to arrange the money. The nurse was kind so risking her own job she gave a day's concession to pay the deposit. Nevertheless, she strictly warned that if Neela did not pay the rupees by the next morning, the treatment of the patient would be stopped. Neela gratefully blessed the nurse and fell into the task right away.

Keeping all the grievances aside, she hastily went into the waiting room to make him arrange the money. But to her wonder, he had already disappeared. She called him on his mobile but it was out of reach. 'Rascal! Putting his own child in the mouth of death, where has he gone?' muttering resentfully, she redialed his number, but again she received the same notification. This event made her nervous. Nonetheless, she tried his number a number of times, but unfortunately, she could not get across him. She remembered the nurse's last warning and for a moment lost her heartbeat. Consequently, now she grew more agitated and while crying and calling him, she ran helter-skelter in and around the hospital in search of him. Some neighbours searched for him at home and even in all the possible daaru addas where he could possibly go. But, they could detect him nowhere.

Time was rapidly elapsing and with it, her worries and fear too. The neighbours, especial women folk were cursing Nava for his outrageous deed and for leaving the child and wife in that critical situation. Now, Neela realized that there was no meaning in spending time on searching for him. All she wanted to do was to save her child at any cost. For a while, she pondered over and as she remembered something, she straightway picked up her mobile and began to dial a number.

Neela and neighbours had mistaken Nava. He had not escaped from the hospital. Actually, he had overheard the nurse's warning and he was now wandering in the market pleading the acquainted traders for lending him money to continue his child's treatment. However, since he was a drunkard, most of the people were not ready to believe in him and those who believed in him were not ready to give him that big amount. Whomever he approached for help was flatly denying his request on some false account. Subsequently, he, being determined to get money, met a cement dealer, told him the mishap and then earnestly appealed to lend him fifteen thousand rupees to save his child. However, like others, the dealer too gave an excuse and showed his inability to help him. Nevertheless, Nava kept on pleading with him for the money. Eventually, the person, being annoyed, got up, slapped in Nava's face and pushed him out of the shop.

For Nava, It was a way to repent for his mistake and he really meant it. After all, he was a father. Although he was a drunkard, his heart was burnt, perhaps as badly as the child was. He did not give up; he rose to his feet thinking to knock at Rakmaji's door and see if he could help.

He swiftly went to Rakmaji's home. But, there he came to know that Rakmaji was at the municipality. However, when he reached the municipality walking 4 k.m. hotfoot, he found him nowhere in the building. He then tried to call him on his mobile number, but he got no response from him. So being anxious, he again and again climbed up and down and peeped in every chamber while dialing and redialing Rakmaji's mobile number, but the result was same. Eventually, on enquiring a peon about him, the peon told him that that day Rakmaji had not come there. On this, for a while he wondered about it, but since he had no much time, he paced to Mitramandal Katta hoping to find the man over there. Soon he reached there huffing and puffing, but it was in vain; he was not there. He then again rolled to Rakmaji's bungalow.

As he approached the house, he found Rakmaji's bike propped up in the foreyard. This sight brought a smile to his face. Since the house was quiet, it seemed the family had collapsed into siesta. So, he knocked at the door softly. And, after a minute or two, a huge lady having fair complexion but a pumpkin like face with a round nose and swollen eyes, opened the door and rigidly asked him 'Why have you come again?' 'Nothing Aakka, just wanted to meet Rakmaji?' 'I told you that he is not at home.' On this, he hesitatingly said, 'But, his bike and shoes are here!' Having realized her own foolishness, she sighed over it and then irritatingly said, 'Yes, he is at home, but now he is sleeping; come afterwards.' 'Aakka, it's very urgent, please wake him up for a while! My child is in hospi...' 'Don't tell me, I know about it. Don't disturb our sleep; you go now,' saying so she closed the door. Even though he felt too bad about it, he cursed himself for his own mistake and sat on the stair helplessly waiting for them to complete their rest.

Gradually, time was splitting and so he was feeling more and more restless. Besides, every now and then, his child's pathetic face was floating on his eyes and its painful scream was echoing in his ears. These two phenomena had set his heart on fire. His soul was urging to flee to his child like a sparrow and sooth it in his arms. But, since he had to manage the amount to save it, until he got the money, he couldn't go. Moreover, he was apprehensive of Rakmaji's going away.

Approximately, after one and half hour, the door creaked and he startlingly sprang up. Seeing him yet there, the woman wondered and asked, 'Have you been here since then?' In reply, he just disarmingly smiled and asked, 'Akka, has he woken up?' 'No' said she rigidly and went inside the house. Since he understood why she had gone inside, he did not amaze at her departure. On the contrary, he suspired with a relief and while gazing at the door he anxiously mumbled, 'Now Rakmaji should quickly agree; no, he won't say no -   since morning I haven't seen my child – come fast

Rakmaji, let me go to my child now! My poor child is alone without me!' In the meantime, as she appeared, he became alert. He thought Rakmaji would be following her. Soon she stood in the door while he looked into the passage behind her expecting Rakmaji's arrival. Having noticed it, she said, 'Yet there is much time for him to wake up.' Saying so she produced an axe and beckoned to him to take it from her stretched hands saying, 'Till then cut those wood logs into small pieces.' However, he did not take the axe. He joined his hands and pleaded her to wake her husband up and also promised that he would cut all the logs the next day. But, she shook her head negatively and said, 'I can't do that; he would shout at me. Anyways, you come tomorrow if you are in a hurry, and if you are going to wait, take this axe and chop the logs.' Now, he had no other option than cutting the logs. He quietly took the axe from her and moved unwillingly towards the pile of logs. That great heap was not going to take less than three hours. On the one hand, the pull of the child was squeezing his heart and on the other, the cunning obligation was blackmailing his helplessness. Owing to his helplessness, he began the work reluctantly, but suddenly his frustration stung him and he became furious: he put his frustration and helplessness against the logs and madly went on striking the axe on them. He kept on breaking log after log without any break. Even though he was breathing short and sweat was pouring off his brow, he stopped neither to breathe deeply nor to wipe off the sweat on his face. Moreover, his eyes had turned red and the body was shivering; tears and sweat were continuously dripping off his chin. In between, he was also chewing his teeth, mumbling something and cursing himself. It seemed as if he was punishing himself for being responsible for his child's pathetic condition.

Almost after one and a half hour, he slackened the grip on the axe.

He was vertically perspired and exhausted. While groaning about his complaining back, he mechanically erected his upper body and went to the door by placing his hands on the waist. Now, the door was open and the house full of guffaws. So, he peeped inside and found two young chaps viewing some mimicry show on TV. He called them twice but they were so engrossed in watching the show that they could not hear his voice. So, next time, he, being tired and frustrated, called them so loudly that both the boys startled and looked in the direction of the sound. The elder boy, being short tempered, minded it and slanged Nava for shouting so loudly. The boy's words filled Nava with humiliation and indignation. Notwithstanding, he suppressed his feelings and calmly asked the boy for Rakmajibau. However, the boy arrogantly denied answering his question and asked him to get lost from the door. But, Nava stood there helplessly. Soon Rakmaji's wife, Aakabai bustled into the hall asking the boy why and whom he was shouting at and after listening to him, she went to the door and roughly asked Nava, 'Why were you shouting unnecessarily?' 'No, i was just calling him!' he then joined his hands and pleaded, 'But, if you feel that I am wrong, please beg me pardon. And, please call Rakmaji; my child is waiting for me in the hospital!' 'But, for what do you want to meet him?' asked she. Since she was very meager and peevish, he tried to avoid her question thinking she might dissuade her husband from giving him money. However, when she insistently asked him the same question again, he couldn't dare to hide the reason from her. He hesitantly said, 'For... my child's treatment I.... need some.... money.' But, on listening to him she did not react harshly. She saw the tears in his eyes and no sooner she went inside the house than she returned with a pouch in her hand. She opened it and while seriously counting the currency notes into it, she casually spoke, 'Haan .. I forgot to tell you; Rakmaji has gone to Solapur for some urgent work.' 'What! When?' uttered he out of shock and sorrow. 'When you were busy in chopping the wood-logs in the backyard,' replied she. On listening to these words, he felt as if he had fallen down from the seventh sky. He remorsefully slapped on his forehead and sat on his haunches holding his head in hands. She then smiled and softly said, 'Hey you donkey! Don't be nervous; get up. Rakmaji has gone and not money. I will give you.' This generous offer relieved him from his agony. A thousand of times, he wholeheartedly blessed and thanked her in a moment. Furthermore, he hastily bristled and gratefully laid his head on her feet saying, 'No friend, no relative and even no God but you did for my child and for me. I will be in your debt throughout my life.' After that, she asked him to leave her feet and stand up, and at once he stood up lowering his head before her. She fished out currency notes from the pouch and while putting them in his hand, she triumphantly said, 'Do you know? Ramya was going to chop the logs for 200 rupees, but I am giving you a hundred rupee extra.' Thereon, he was bewildered and terrified. Nevertheless, he smiled disarmingly and while handing over the money back to her, he calmly said, 'No Aakka, I don't want wages for chopping the logs.' However, she refused to take the money and made him keep it for himself. She then calmly asked him, 'You don't want money; what do you want then?' 'Aakka, I want your help — for God's sake, lend me fifteen thousand rupees to save my child!' 'Fifteen thousand?' she nonchalantly confirmed the amount with him and while looking into her pouch, she signalled him to give her the money in his hand. Before returning the money, he threw a glance at her face and grew apprehensive, as she looked stern. She took the money from his hand, pulled out a hundred rupee note from the amount and thrust the remaining two hundred rupee notes into his hand saying, 'You deserve only this much. Being good to you is not at all affordable – you people will suck us dry. Do you think Rakmaji has opened a charitable bank; at once hail your tail away from my door!' She then briskly went inside and slammed the door shut on his face.

Being shattered he looked in the direction of his way with his tearful eyes and helplessly dragged himself forward with the heart palpitating with fear and head buzzing with intense self-indignation. In between, he suddenly stopped and whispered, 'Yes, I don't deserve!' and took some strange way that led towards the setting sun.

Here, Neela was also in a predicament. It was almost evening, yet, despite imploring almost every relative and acquaintance to help, she had got no assurance of relief from any of them. The trepidation had vertically shaken her up now. All the time, she was sobbing and inwardly invoking Goddess, Lakshmiaie for help. Indeed, she was undergoing the greatest stress and agonies of her life.

In the meantime, her mobile rang. As she picked it up, her dried lips parted into a broad smile and her pale face brightened up. She lavishly spoke the words of blessing and gratefulness. Putting the mobile down, she sighed happily and dialed her husband's number. However, it was yet out of coverage. This made her more furious. 'Son of witch! In which hell is he lying?' she shouted.

In fact, her cousin sister who lived in Pune had managed the money for her, but someone had to go to Pune for collecting it from her. Now, who would go was the question. There were some neighbours with her, but Somya, being her cousin brother, stepped forward to go and with him his friend Sanjya too.

That very evening, they caught the intercity train and by 10 pm, they reached at the cousin sister's house. On the cousin's insistence for supper, they had it, took the money and without further delay bade her farewell. They hastily reached the Pune Station, but on inquiring, they came to know that yet there were two hours for the passenger to arrive. So, they sat on the platform waiting for the train. They talked a bit on the magnificence of the city and then fell into silence. Sitting over there, they were passively viewing all the activities at the station. However, all the while both of them were feeling some sort of restlessness – as if that day they had missed something. But, being aware of the present situation, they had sat with tight lips. After an hour, Sanjya, being unable to cope up with the anxiety, broke up the hesitation and said, 'I am feeling a strange agitation. I think, it is because this evening we missed our daily dose, didn't we?' 'Without it I am too feeling so agitated as a fish feels without water!' said Somya and then sighing sadly he spoke further, 'But, I don't have money for it; I mean I have, but just for buying our tickets. And, let me tell you clearly; at any cost I can't touch that fifteen thousand. That is to save my niece.' Having minded Somya's dry words, Sanjya felt heartburn, so he grumpily asked him, 'Is this the reward of my friendship?' He continued loudly, 'Seeing you and your sister in a trouble no one but I accompanied you at the cost of losing my today's wages.' This attracted other passengers' attention. Some of the curious passengers began to take interest in them expecting them to be a good aid of passing their time while waiting for their trains. 'How could you even think that I will make you touch that money?' he pompously shouted at Somya. Now, Somya, who had been calm so far, just stared at him angrily and Sanjya sat quietly. The disappointed passengers then dispersed while sighing and clicking their tongues.

After sometime, Sanjya stood up and said, 'I am going.' 'Where?' asked annoyed Somya. 'I have seventy rupees. If you wish, come with me; we will have half-half and come back here again within five minutes.' For a moment, he pondered over Sanjya's offer and after finding nothing wrong in it, he positively nodded his head.

Subsequently, in search of a local wine house, they entered a nearby pell-mell area and soon found one. Before entering the wine adda, Somya strictly warned Sanjya that they had to have only a bottle and not more than that. Sanjya happily agreed with him. Then, they bought a bottle from the counter and went inside the wine adda. Sanjya impatiently opened the bottle, poured half of the liquor into a glass for Somya and in no time, he devoured the wine of his share. Somya too finished his glass and grunted contentedly. 'Haa..! Brain vibrated. It's a real thing -pure and strong!' Sanjya exclaimed while smacking his lips. 'Is it necessary to buy railway-tickets?' asked Somya while leaning to his left side. 'not at all; many people travel without tickets' Sanjya answered at once. To this, Somya announced with heavy tongue, 'Sanjya, we will go without tickets but we will have one-one bottle each.' This was all what Sanjya wanted. He cheered Somya saying, 'Oh my bravo! Indeed, you are the only man on this land.' Then, taking money from Somya, he walked towards the counter, but in the midway, he remembered something, so he stopped there for a moment swaying back and forth and then instead of going to the counter, he went back to Somya. He seriously asked Somya, 'What I say; why to go by train?' 'How to go then?' asked Somya dizzily. 'Bravo, we will go by plane; that is also without tickets!' shouted Sanjya gleefully and moved towards the counter. At that time, Somya shouted, 'Hey Sanjya, bring three; one for the pilot – we will give it to him and ask to drop us directly at Sathe Nagae.' 'Oh my tiger! You simply snatched my words' saying so Sanjya went to the counter and returned with three bottles. They did not know when they finished the last bottle. Thereafter, their thirst and trance kept on increasing. Soon the wine stung their consciousness and made them entirely indifferent to the whole world. Sanjya then unsteadily rose to his feet and stuttered, 'Come with me I will show you the real glamour of the city.' Somya too somehow managed to arise and tailed Sanjya towards the main road. While walking zigzag with uncontrolled steps, they were insanely howling, sprawling, and giving a good laugh to the people in the street. In the meantime, Sanjya suddenly lost his balance and collapsed having Somya toppled over him. Sanjya lay by his belly and Somya piled on him like a dead body. Lying in that position, they sang, cried, spoke rubbish things and eventually slept as they were.

LAYER – 11

The day broke. Neela, fixing her swollen eyes to the road, had been standing in the porch since predawn. Somya was expected to come by 5 to 5:30 am but he had not come yet. She was aware of the fact that the hospital had already given her relaxation so it would not tolerate further delay in the payment. For this reason, she was little anxious and as the day advanced, her anxiety kept on intensifying. She wished to make a phone call to Somya, but unfortunately, neither Somya nor Sanjya had a mobile. Eventually, she called her cousin sister and asked about them, but she told the same as she had told her at night that they were coming by the passenger train departing at 12 am. However, when she told Neela that the train might be late, she felt little relieved. Now, she stood gazing at the road with hopeful eyes while praying Goddess, Laximiaie in the mind to enable Somya reach before the doctor's round.

In the east, the innocent sun was gradually metamorphosing into its furious adulthood. Shops were opened; people were rushing towards their destinations; on the road, vehicles were plying helter-skelter and Somya and Sanjya, being unaware of all these, were deep in their dreamless slumber – lying on the road like unknown dead bodies. Fortunately, a kind driver blew the horn shrilly and Somya startled awoke to it. Being puzzled, he looked around: he was on the main road; Sanjya was lying beside him; vehicles and people were passing by their either sides and the people standing at the bus stop were looking at them. He was in utter confusion. He did not remember when and how he reached there. In between, as he suddenly remembered something, he hurriedly stood up and hastily checked his pockets. However, to his surprise there was nothing in the pockets. This notice sent a shudder through him and the thought of its evil-consequence ruined him. He sorrowfully slapped his forehead and falling on his haunches began moaning about the lost money. 'For God's sake, return my rupees!' he pleaded people. Hearing Somya's hullabaloo Sanjya awoke and like Somya, he too got puzzled over the present situation. Somya then went to the footpath and started asking every passerby the only question, 'Have you taken fifteen thousand rupees from my pocket?' In reply, he received slaps, slangs, scolding, mockery and humiliation. Nevertheless, he crazily kept on running after people and stopping them for asking about his money.

Standing under a tree Sanjya was passively watching it. 'He seems to be a lunatic escaped from some mental hospital,' said someone standing next to him but he said nothing about it. Now, Somya's lips and throat had dried up; his clothes were wet with sweat; the body was fatigued and voice was cracked. 'Fifteen thousand! For God's sake return it or else I will kill myself here!' he spoke indistinctly and stood resting his forehead onto a streetlight-post. For a while, he stood still closing his eyes and all of a sudden, he opened his eyes and forcefully banged his own head on the post. And, in frustration he kept on colliding his head again and again with the pole. Seeing this, Sanjya and some people quickly ran and drew him away from the pole. The collision had caused several cracks on his head. Out of those cracks, a number of streams of blood were gushing and rolling down his neck, nose, cheeks and chin. In order to stop the bleeding Sanjya put off his shirt and tied it around Somya's head. Then, a kind man immediately took Somya to a government hospital by his car and after bandaging his injured head dropped them at the railway station.

Every now and then, the nurse was calling Neela and demanding for the payment, but every time Neela was giving her the only excuse that the train was late and her brother was on the way. In the morning, she had assured that her brother would come by afternoon; in the afternoon she told that he would come by 6 pm and now she told her that her brother was on the way and he would be in the hospital just within an hour. But now the nurse had no more patience. She was tired of listening to her same cat and bull story. 'People like you deserve no help; you would swallow my job!' she irritatingly said and went to the doctor's cabin to report him about this case. Soon the doctor called her and asked to take her child to some municipal hospital. But, she sank to her knees in supplication and by joining her hands implored, 'Doctor Sahib! For God's sake, don't say that. Please don't leave my child to die! Have mercy upon my child. I will b.....' 'Neela, please stop it,' the doctor interrupted her and continued, 'Everyday I deal with agonies and cries, death and birth, so don't try to blackmail me in the name of humanity.' On this, although the doctor kept on hesitating and warning her to be away, she rested her head on his feet and begged for her child's life. Eventually, the doctor sighed and said to her, 'See, this is not a charitable hospital. So far what we have done is more than humanity. I am going to wait for two more hours, but after that, if he does not come by then, you will have to leave this hospital with your child in whichever condition it might be. Agree?' 'Yes' said she and left sobbing.

Standing in the corridor, Neela was helplessly waiting for Somya with the eyes over-brimmed with tears. The misfortune had heavily fallen upon her. Her child was struggling for life in the ICU;

the husband had disappeared since the previous day. In addition, if the bill was not paid by the given time, the doctor was going to stop the treatment. The time limit given for paying the bill was about to end and yet there was no sign of Somya's arrival.   She was not getting what to do if Somya would not come by that time. With every passing moment, the flames of worries and fear were escalating more and more and wolfing her down bit by bit. In the meantime, her neighbour, Ranubai arrived there with some food for Neela. She affectionately stroked her back and insisted her to have the food. However, Neela refused to eat and broke down. 'Soma hasn't come yet; now the doctor is going to discharge my child as it is. You tell me, what should I do now?' said she while breathing half. 'At once you alone run off stealthily from here,' Ranubai advised her. However, Neela was shocked to listen to her. She did not like even a bit of it. 'No, at any cost I won't do it leaving my baby here,' Neela clearly told her. 'It's better to let the baby be in the care of hospital than taking it to home in a half alive condition and waiting for its death,' saying so Ranubai took Neela's hand in hers and assured, 'Listen to me, instead of waiting here in vainly, go out and arrange the bill or find out Somya.' 'But, the doctor?' 'The doctor cannot discharge your baby and hand it over to anyone else except for its close relatives.' Now, Neela seemed convinced. She nodded yes. She then peeped into the ICU through the door-glass; saw her child with wet eyes and burning heart and from the rare door of the hospital disappeared in the darkness while sobbing.

At the very night, Jaya, after feeding her children with supper, sent them to bed. She then arranged the cooking place and went to sleep without having her dinner even though she had had nothing since morning. Lying beside the children, she was trying to sleep, but the moment she would close her eyes, the hateful face of Raja would drift in her eyesight and his words would echo in her ears. Eventually, she moved up and sat propping her back against the wall to avoid this sleepless nightmare. In fact, since that incident, this was almost a daily affair. Sometimes, she would spend a wakeful night shoring her back against the wall. She had lost her mental peace. She had become speechless, ill tempered and dry in behaviour and so the children too were deeply affected by the sudden change in their mother's conduct. They were afraid to ask or tell her anything. They would neither go out to play nor dare to play in the house. All the time, they would sit individually in different corners of the house either fiddling with a toy or flipping pages of a book. That's why, the house had lost its liveliness and appeared like a deserted place.

Now, it was quarter to eleven. Jaya had freaked out of sitting, so, at that odd time, she collected the used utensils in a big container, took them to the foreyard and began to wash them. Her hands were scrubbing and washing utensils, but her eyes were fixed somewhere else looking in void and the mind was profoundly engrossed in some thoughts. In a way, there was no sync between her actions and thoughts. In the meantime, she abruptly leaped onto her feet as Raja's face flashed in her sight. To cast out his image from her eyes, she sprinkled water on the eyes. However, the image was yet in her sight. It made her dazed and petrified. 'It's reality or hallucination?' she whispered and stood still gazing at him. 'What happened? Has a snake bitten you?' these rough articulations of Raja blew her illusion to smithereens and electrified her whole body with fear. After awaking to this bitter reality, her condition was like a mouse, which comes face to face with a cobra. However, this time, she did not want him to do anything unpleasant with her. So, she hid her fear and boldly asked him, 'Why have you come here now? At once get lost from my yard!' 'I think you are weird of your conjugal life, aren't you?' he mischievously uttered. 'I say go or I will gather people!' she shouted and hastily began to put both the washed and unwashed utensils in the container. In the meanwhile, he took out a bottle of daaru and finished it in one go. As the alcohol sent vibrations to his brain, he shook his head and stood motionless for a while. But, once the alcohol mixed in his blood, he became bold. He caught her wrist and shouted, 'Shout and call the people; let them know what I had done with you; let them spread it everywhere – to your in-laws ; let your children awake and later tell your husband what had happen to you!' These words subdued her. Feeling the gravity of his words, she became aware of its evil-consequences. Now, she could no more sustain her fake boldness. 'But you had said only once; now for God's sake leave me!' pleaded she in a cracked voice. On this, he dramatically laughed and said, 'I don't remember what I say or do in the trance of wine. So forget about it' and then sternly warned her, 'But, now you remember; whenever I feel I will come here, and if you try to protest like this, I will ruin you and your family.' Saying so, he forcefully pulled her behind him by her wrist towards the house while she kept on appealing him to leave her.

Approximately, at 1 am, the Mumbai-Sholapur passenger halted at the Pune Station. This time, Somya and Sanjya succeeded in entering the train furtively and somehow managed to reach at Kurdwadi without tickets. They were hungry and tired. Since Somya was feeling very weak, he was walking haltingly like a bedridden patient. Fortunately, no TC noticed them on the platform, so they came out of the junction safely. However, their destination was yet 35 km away from this place and to reach there they had to travel either by bus or by jeep. But, the problem with these conveyances was unlike the passenger train, there was no scope to go by them without money or tickets. Hence, how to go to Barshi was a puzzle for them to solve now.

Now, slowly the objects merged in the darkness of night were taking shapes. In the dim sky, white flocks of cranes were gliding in an arch form while quacking turn wise. Awaking to this quacking alarm, the cocks too had begun to blow their morning sirens. At some houses, the sounds of pouring water and clanging of utensils were heard and from some distant temple, aarti accompanied with clapping and the clinking of a bell was being heard.

Now, they reached the station gate. Just outside of the gate on its right, the recently deboarded passengers had crowded a snack-cart. Actually, the aroma of bhaji (pakoda) was appetizing people and attracting them towards that cart. Having exhausted by the tedious journey, people were replenishing themselves by feasting on this street-treat. Someone was having poha; someone was taking a mouthful bite of vadapav and someone was sipping hot tea with hot bhaji and samosas while those two empty bellies were staring at the eaters with hungry eyes. 'I think pakodas seem very tasty!' said Sanjya and heavily sniffed the aroma of pakodas. 'God knows how and when we would go to Barsi - I feel I will die of hunger here,' spoke Somya in a feeble voice. Then, Sanjya went to the cart. There were many customers before him, but not in a row. Every one of them was trying to get his order first. However, the cart-owner alone was handling them. His hands and head were working like a machine; at a time, he was serving food, giving and taking money and listening to the orders too. 'Two plates of bhaji and two of vadapav' Sanjya ordered when two others were hastening for theirs. The owner speedily served plates to three of them and began to work on the next orders. The first two customers gave money while Sanjya took the plates and sat on the bench at the cart. Seeing the plates, Somya came hotfoot and joined Sanjya. They were so hungry that Just in a few minutes, they emptied the plates. Now, they were feeling better. Sanjya sighed ecstatically and then worriedly asked his mate, 'Now bill?' But, Sanjya remained calm and quiet. 'Sanjya, the owner is busy; let's slip away from here fast,' Somya whispered. On this, Sanjya stood up and then Somya too being ready to move. However, instead of decamping from there stealthily, to Somya's amazement, Sanjya went to the cart and stood right in front of the owner. The owner took a glance over him and hastily but politely asked him, 'Yes Sahib, what would you like to eat?' 'Money' said Sanjya firmly. To this, the owner raised his head from the work in his hand and looked at him strangely. Sanjya then explained him, 'I mean, just before some time, I took double plates of vadapav and bhaji means pakode giving you a hundred rupee note, but then you did not return my remaining money.' The owner then stressed on his memory to recollect it, but, since many customers had given him hundred rupee notes, he could make out nothing, besides he had other customers to attend. So, doubting his own memory and believing in what the customer said, without wasting any more time, he handed over money to Sanjya and while smiling disarmingly apologized for the inconvenience. 'Oh forget about it; I have forgiven you' said Sanjya calmly. He then picked up a pakoda from the container saying, 'But indeed! Your mart deserves a visit again' and chuckling secretly to Somya walked towards the bus stand while eating the pakoda in his hand.

Thus, after managing the food and fair of the bus, they had now to arrange fifteen thousand rupees after going to Barsi. For this reason, Somya was overwhelmingly tense though Sanjya had assured him that Rakmaji would help them. Soon, they got on a bus and within an hour reached their hometown. From the bus stand, they directly went to Rakmaji's bungalow. However, it was yet asleep. So, Sanjya, with little hesitation, knocked at the door. After sometime, Rakmaji's wife opened the door and on seeing Somya's bandaged head, she directly started scolding them thinking that they had fought with someone and now they had come to seek her husband's help in their affair. Sanjya tried to clarify, but before he could utter the second letter of his first word, she quietened him and asked them to be off from there. Fortunately, at that time, Rakmaji came there and after seeing Somya and Sanjya, he beckoned to his wife to go in. He then asked them what the matter was. In response to him, Somya recounted, 'Rakmaji, my niece is struggling for her life in the ICU. For her treatment my sister had borrowed money from a cousin sister who lives in Pune, and we both had gone to fetch it. But on the train, someone stole it from my pocket.' 'Then go to the police station and report about it. Why did you come here?' shouted Rakmaji's wife from behind the door. 'Are you yet there? At once go inside,' shouted Rakmaji irritatingly and said to Somya, 'Actually, she is right. Go to the police station.' Somya then joined his hands and said, 'Rakmajibhua, for God's sake save my niece!' 'My husband is not a doctor or a God to save the child; go to a temple or a doctor,' shouted the lady being unable to resist herself from interfering. Then, Rakmaji, being exasperated, slapped his forehead and finally took them to the backyard so that they could speak comfortably.

Rakmaji understood why they had come to him and clearly told them that if they had come to borrow money from him, they should not waste their time there. On listening to these straightforward words, both of them looked at each other and remained quiet for a while. Thereafter, Sanjya sheepishly suggested Rakmaji that as that day he had lent money to Jagtap Dada and Jadhav Anna on interest, he should lent it Somya too on interest. But, Rakmaji told him that Jatap Dada and Jadhav Anna were farmers. They had their lands as mortgage. Jadhav Anna had only an acre of land, but its market value was forty lacks. He then asked Sanjya what Somya had and added that even the land where Somya lived was of the municipality. However, Sanjya guaranteed him that Somya would repay his loan, but Rakmaji laughed and told him that he did not think so. For a long time, Somya had been mutely bearing his words, but this time in a raised voice, he told Rakmaji that if he thought so about him, he should also not be too much sure of Jadhav Anna. Rakmaji did not like it. So, he glared at him and asked what he meant to say. Somya knew that Rakmaji did not like if anyone challenged his words, yet he boldly replied him that sometimes even the biggest businessperson like Vijay Maliya fails to repay loans and farmers commit suicide for the same. Listening to this dialogue, Rakmaji laughed at Somya and ridiculed him saying that his logic was very funny. Further, he told Somya that he knew better how to recover money from a borrower and he was not generous like government to free a businessperson from his debt. He also told him that even if a farmer commits suicide, a money lender like him need not to worry about his money, because the government, media and almost everyone in the society is very sensitive to such suicides. The government gives a relief fund to the farmer's family. Thus, there is a substantial assurance of getting his returns.

Somya then convincingly told him that he would regularly work day and night and would pay off his loan along with the interest. But, Rakmaji was not at all convinced. On the contrary, he cynically questioned Somya who would give him work regularly. However, Somya had no answer, so he remained mute. But Sanjya took the turn and promptly answered that Somya was a member of the government's Rojgar Hami scheme. So, if he did not get a job on a day, he would get wages for the day. Besides, his mother got six hundred rupees per month under Niradhar scheme.

However, this poor advocacy of Sanjya could only coax Rakmaji' s laughter. 'Six hundred per month! So heavy amount!' said Rakmaji ironically while controlling his laughter and asked Somya if his mother could manage a month with that money. In reply, the answerer nodded no. Further, Rakmajibuau like a professional lender, asked Somya if the wages that he got under the Rojagahami scheme were sufficient to run his family and most importantly whether they were paid on time. This time too Somya preferred being quiet to telling lies, because he knew that Rakmajibhua daily spent almost whole day in the municipal office, so he knew very well how those schemes were executed.

Subsequently, Rakmaji sighed and resentfully asked, 'Somya, you have neither an assured employment nor any property for mortgage, then how will you return my money?' For a minute, he waited for Somya's answer and after a minute's silence, he continued, 'Even if a destitute worker like you commits suicide, no one takes its notice; even a dog never barks. You better understand that even your death can't pay my debt.' The last words pinched on Somya's heart. For a moment, he felt to pull Rakmaji down and grab hold of his throat until he died. But, being needy, his anger was handicapped and hence he stood helplessly having self-disgust in his eyes and the burden of infinite poverty on his dropped head and shoulder.

After that, Rakmaji spoke, 'See, even a bank does not sanction a loan without mortgage, then how you expect me to lend you money without any assurance.' 'Will my house do?' asked Somya softly. 'Hun! I don't know, what do I do with it? But anyways, bring a 100 rupee notary stamp' saying so Rakmaji went into the house.

In the morning, Neela, being agitated to see her child, reached hospital. When a ward boy noticed her arrival, he dropped the mob in his hand and ran towards the doctor's cabin. Seeing this, she swiftly ran into the hospital and began to climb the stairs. While climbing the stairs, she heard some familiar voice crying mournfully, so she climbed the stairs more rapidly with a rabbit's heart. However, on hitting the floor, she found that the lamenting was coming from the general ward located on the first end of the floor and not from the ICU ward situated on another end   of   the storey. Now, she was tremendously relieved. She sighed happily and walked hotfoot towards the ICU. On the way, while passing by the door of the general ward, she took a glance over the scene inside and when she was just about to cross the door, a man from the crowd turned his face towards the door and her pacing legs stopped. She jerked herself backwards and reconfirmed the face: it was of her husband's friend, Kishya. When he saw her, he gave her a sympathetic look and passed by her without a word. This reminded her of her husband who had been unseen for the last two days. In a fraction of a second a hundred different thoughts lashed her brain. Now, her heart began to palpitate unusually, however, she darted towards the crowd keeping her hand on the chest. She pushed people aside and saw: her child, closing its tiny eyes, was lying on its father's lap. Uninterrupted by the din made by its father, it had slept calmly forever. When she perceived the matter, she screamed and abruptly collapsed on the floor. She became unconscious. Someone quickly sprinkled water on her face and she gained consciousness. The setback of her child's death made her so agonized that she banged her head on the floor, wailed painfully and kept on weeping bitterly.

After a while, while crying she stood up and snatched the child from Nava's lap saying, 'You giant! You have only eaten up my child for your daaru! Now, you are no one of mine, not even my enemy!'

Now, almost all the kith and kin had gathered. Some of the men quickly arranged things required for the funeral. Thus, before the child could understand life and before it could step towards the future and explore life, it was on the last ride to the graveyard and perhaps this fact was pinching Neela's heart. All the way, she was mourning and calling her dead son back to life. She was again and again invoking Goddess Lakshmi to return her child. While, Nava was remorsefully sobbing and in between tearing his own hair or slapping in his own face. Soon the procession reached at the child's ultimate destination – before its arrival, a pit had been dug out. Placing the baby beside the pit, the menfolk besieged the pit for the burial ceremony. One of the men came forth, applied kumkum to the baby's forehead, offered some flowers, burnt incense-sticks and then chanted a particular hymn to invoke Lord Shiva for giving the child's soul shelter in Kailash Lok. Thereafter, he asked the mother and father to put something precious in the child's mouth. Since Nava had nothing to give his child, he stood still shedding tears and cursing his own fate for not having even a last gift for his dear son. However, Neela, with a jerk, broke the mangalsutra that hung about her neck; pulled all three gold beads out of it and gave them to the man. The man put the beads in the child's mouth and unwrapping its face completely, said, 'Nava, Neela, have a last glance over your child – afterwards you will nowhere see it again.' The last words pierced the parents' hearts. Nava embraced the baby and broke down loudly. The mother too scrambled to see and give a last hug to her dearest departing son. She held the kid in her arms; showered the thin face with kisses and then holding it against her chest, she went on weeping acrimoniously. Subsequently, the man interrupted her, took the child from her and putting it in the pit, pushed a heap of soil into the pit. In no time, the little face in the mother's gazing eyes disappeared forever under the heap of soil.

It was evening, but there was no usual hustle bustle. Houses were speechless, TVs and DVD players were unheard, foreyards and even roads were empty. So the area around Nava's house seemed gloomy. Nava, sitting alone in a corner of his dark house, was looking outside through the door in void. In between, having recalled his child's memories, he was sobbing. His child's mirthful laughter and his wife's rush to do things in the house would make the house happening and alive. But now, he was all alone; except dead silence and darkness there was nothing at his home. For the first time he felt so lonely that he thought there was no shoulder in the world for him to rest his head and cry. 'Nava, why are you sitting in the darkness?' this question of Raja broke down Nava's trance of thoughts. Raja, Sanjya, Chandya and Somya entered the house, sat beside him and tried to console him. After sometime, Raja asked him to go out with them, however, Nava refused to do so. But despite his protest, everyone insisted on him to join them. Finally, he had to give up his stance.

They took him to Devya's daaru adda and insisted on him to take just a glass of daaru with them. Here also they made him accept their offer. Thus, he had one glass and after that, he did not say no to their offers. To give him solace, even other drunkards in the daaru adda offered him a glass of wine and he kept on consuming one after the other.

As alcohol spread in him, his expressions of sorrow flared up in more and more dramatic manner. Sometimes he would cry for his child and all of a sudden he would start slanging and cursing Rakmaji and his wife, and then he would again cry like a child saying 'Neele, don't leave me alone! Come home, or I will die!' Listening to his elegy, an old drunkard approached Nava, kissed on his forehead and hugging Nava tightly, blew his siren of cry. In between, someone came shouting, 'run away, police has come!' Hearing the announcement, the people in the adda ran away in different directions while the old man, being unaware of this affair, kept on wailing and crying painfully holding Nava against his chest. However, when he heard the word 'police', at once he stopped his siren and with a frightened face, he struggled to detach himself from Nava's arms. Nevertheless, Nava kept on crying and clinging to the old chap's shoulder like a child. Eventually, the man gave a nasty bite on Nava's arm and getting himself freed from the clutch, he made one bound in the air.

Soon three policemen barged into the shed. Devya had already kept their monthly installment ready. Without having any sort of dialogue, they took the money and left in the manner they had come.

Escaping from daaru adda, Raja directly reached Jaya's house carrying a mug of wine in his hand. In the yard, Jaya's children were engrossed in playing and inside the house, she was busy in cooking. In the meantime, Jaya heard knocking at the door and assuming one of her children at the door, she softly said 'Bala, do not bang the door'. But, again there was a knock on the door. This time she got angry and while looking up, she briskly shouted 'you rude chil..' and finding Raja at the door she gobbled up her words and was goggle-eyed at the finding. She dropped the vessel in her hand and joining her hands implored, 'For God's sake, go – my children ar...' 'Shut your mouth up' cutting her words, he shouted and then asking her to keep the mug of wine in the house mischievously added 'keep awake, tonight I am coming!' However, when she didn't move to take the mug, he threatened her of entering the house and doings the things that she did not want her children to see. At last, being vulnerable to his threat, she reluctantly took the mug.

Now the election was around the corner. There was a neck-to-neck competition between Jhople Sahib and Khaut Sahib, so the promotion rallies of both the parties were in full swing. Both the parties were lavishly spending money on mutton, wine, orchestra, hoardings and other public stunts.

One night, around at 10 pm, a car entered Sathe Nagar and halted at Mitramandal Katta. The arrival of the car in the area, caused a sensation and in a minute, curious inhabitants especially urchins clustered around the car to see who the Sahib had come. The door opened and a person, with a moderate height and physique in an extreme white and starched Nehru shirt –pyjama emitting phenomenal fragrance, descended off the car and stood joining his hands with a warm smile on his face. Looking at him, people were flabbergasted; they burst into whispers – 'Hey! He is Khandu's son, Papya!' 'Yes, he is Papya!' 'How he has changed, he doesn't seem to be one of us!' 'So long where had he been?' 'He has become an English professor.' 'His father was too poor.' Then he began to greet and talk to people in the crowd by calling them individually. One of the men arranged chairs for Prof. Praful and his three companions and humbly requested them to sit. Having sat, Praful requested the people to sit down and then began to tell them the intention of his visit. He clearly told them that he had not come there just to beat the drum of his own party or to deliver a long persuasive speech for grabbing their votes, but to awake them from their profound sleep to the reality.

He asked them if they remembered Dr Baba Sahib Ambedkar. In response to his question, almost all the people said yes; some of them even nagged and grumbled saying, 'Are we so ignorant?' 'Is this a question to ask?' and so on. He apologized them for offending their feelings and seeking their permission, he asked them one more question: 'When do we celebrate Ambedkar Jayanti?' '14th April' roared the crowd no sooner than he finished the last word. He applauded their spirit and proposed to answer his last question. On this, a man in the crowd jollily asked, 'Sir, is it a Kon Banega Karowdpati show?' and the crowd giggled. 'No, I think, sir is taking our class,' replied someone from the crowd only. Smilingly thanking to the man for answering on his behalf, Praful asked the mob, 'What did Dr Baba Sahib Ambedkar tell us to do?' However, this time the mob remained silent. After a while, a young man stood up and answered, 'Actually, he told many things.' 'Well my young friend, tell me only one thing.' 'Why not: he told us to fight for our right' 'Do you mean 'Learn, unite and struggle for your right'?' 'Yes' 'You are right but don't forget the preceding words of his preaching 'Learn' and 'unite'. In reaction to this, someone said 'If we knew so much, we would be you, wouldn't we?' On this, Praful smiled and said, 'We do not know is the only problem. I am happy for your love for Baba Sahib. It is good that every year, you celebrate his jayanti to express your gratitude towards him. But brothers, he would really be the happiest if you knew what he actually wanted you to do. In true sense, his efforts would have succeeded if you had followed his words.' 'Hey Mr.! What do you mean by this?' interrupted a man from the crowd obnoxiously. However, no one from the crowd supported him so Praful continued, 'Brothers, I am also one of you but the only difference between you and me is I knew his preaching and I followed it in my life, and the result is here.

Brothers, Dr. B.R.Ambedkar struggled throughout his life simply to open all doors of opportunities for the downtrodden like us. He did everything to give us equality and proper treatment in the society and to sustain it, he told us, "Learn, unit and struggle for your right." However, unfortunately we failed to follow his words. Even these days, instead of educating your children, you send them to wash cups and saucers, to make bricks, to carry containers of soil, and to clean others' houses. For a glass of wine and a plate of Biryani, some of you run after cunning people like Rakmaji and Jhople saying 'Sahib, Sahib,' raising their banners, shouting slogans and giving votes to those corrupt opportunists. That is why, we are yet unable to rise above this poor and miserable living. We have hardly moved away from the point we had started our journey. Let me tell you my friends that by doing this you are simply forwarding poverty to your next generation. On the contrary, selfish politicians like Jhople have been monopolizing opportunities and inheriting them to their next generations. Resultantly, poor people like us are being deprived of opportunities and so yet we are poor.

Although, a way back India emancipated itself from the British Rule, you are still slaves; slaves of poverty, wine, ignorance, superstitions and of those cunning politicians. My friends, rise up; this is the time to change our present and future. And to do so, people like Jhople who were born with a silver spoon in the mouth can never reach to our problems. They cannot empathize our pains. For that, we need someone from us, however, being from us does not mean an immoral and illiterate person like Rakmaji. We need someone who would ethically and responsibly work for the community and country.

My friends I am an ignited mind, entered politics not for baking my own bread but with a centered objective of emancipating my people from poverty, hunger, helplessness and ignorance. I assure you if you give me an opportunity, I would be certainly successful to execute my objective. My friends, I have shared my words neither to win your sympathy nor to bag your votes but to make you understand the importance of education and the corrupt system."

After the speech, everywhere there was silence; even nobody clapped. In the mean time, Shankar Aappa, a kind and supportive person of the area, stood up in the crowd and said, "Bappa, we are proud of you! And all of us are with you." Then everyone started saying, "Go ahead, we are with you...!" and they repeatedly kept on saying so.

LAYER - 19

These days Nava was feeling very lonely. His house appeared utter deserted without his child and wife. In a neutral condition, he would never show even a trace of sorrow on his face but in the trance of wine, he would cry bitterly for his child and wife. He had stopped working. Day and night, he was just consuming alcohol selling whatever bags and baggages he had at home. Now he was not sharing wine with his friends too, so they fought with him and finally boycotted him. He was simply drinking and lying inside the house on the dusty floor where he would spit, urinate, vomit and sometimes in the trance, would relieve himself in his pants. Sometime in the mid night, he would wail and cry painfully. Gradually, his physique was drastically collapsing. His deeply sunken eyes had turned yellowish, tummy had bulged unnaturally, his neck, legs and hands appeared thin like bamboo sticks. All those gave his body a look of a disproportionate figure.

For the whole month, he had been following the same routine. But now there was nothing in the house to sell. His physical condition had increasingly deteriorated; even to go up to

Hagandari, he walked with a great difficulty. His wife had left him forever, friends had boycotted him and neighbours were annoyed of him due to his regular hue and cry. So, nobody was bothered about his illness. After a few days, he was not able to move for his tummy had swelled up like a balloon. In fact, due to the consecutive consumption of alcohol, his liver was severely damaged.

Now, day and night he had been lying in the bed while producing agonized commotions and wailing "Water... Water, Food... Food..." For a few days some of the compassionate neighbours gave him food and water but soon they felt it burdensome so they too started neglecting him. For the next three days, nobody went to see him or to give him water or food. The helpless being, day and night, kept on pleading, "Someone give me water, I am dying... Give me water.... Water...!" but no one listened to him.

Now, regularly Jaya was being exploited by Raja. Every day, Raja would keep a mug of wine at her house and at night he would drink it and throughout night he would not let her sleep.

One day in the trance of wine, Raja was driving the rickshaw and while turning on a corner he dashed the rickshaw to an electric pole. However, fortunately, the collision was moderate. So, except a trivial damage to the rickshaw, everything was fine. But, when the owner of the rickshaw came across the damage, he cancelled Raja's rickshaw-ship and gave it to another person. Later, Raja went door to door of rickshaw owners to get a rickshaw-ship but nowhere there was a vacancy for him. Because of this Raja had to eat whatever his wife would bring from the working place. Most of the time, the food would be stale and insufficient. In those days, he was craving for meat and wine, but it was in vain.

One evening Raja was lying on the cot while watching TV at home. Then, a boy came and told him that Rakmaji Bhau had asked Raja to come at Mitramandal Karta at once. Thinking there might be some serious matter, he hurriedly went there. But on reaching there, he found no hustle-bustle or any crowd. Rakmaji Bhau was sitting alone on the Katta and beside him there were three mugs of wine and a plate of fried beef. As soon as Raja reached at the Katta, Rakmaji said, 'Laka (hai) how long I have been waiting for you! Come fast and join me!' In the beginning Raja superficially hesitated saying, 'carry on Bhau, carry on,' and then went and sat beside him. Rakmaji himself filled a glass for Raja and said, 'Raja, today not to hesitate, drink as much as you want. And, this is not only for today, as long as this Rakmaji Bhau is alive, you will never sleep without wine. And if I don't keep my words, you publicly declare that Rakmaji is not the son of a single father!' 'Rakmaji, please don't say that! In fact I don't understand how to express my gratitude towards you. Bhau, if you command me, this Raja won't hesitate even to die for you!" grateful Raja exclaimed and gulped the second glass of wine. Rakmaji glided the plate of meat towards Raja and beckoned to him to eat. Since Raja had not eaten meat for many days, he happily nodded his head and swallowed pieces after pieces voraciously. "Then Raja, how is going on with your mistress, Jaya?" Suddenly Rakmaji interrogated cunningly. This unexpected question made Raja perplexed, the non-swallowed morsel got stuck in his throat and caused him a series of severe cough. While he coughed, saliva streaked through his mouth and water from his eyes and nose dripped in the plate. In order to give him relief Rakmaji ran his right hand on Raja's back and instead of water he gave another glass of wine saying 'My dear brother take it easy!' Raja gulped it and felt his ribs with his hands to ensure the relief from the cough. 'No, you haven't done anything wrong but what I ask, why are you hiding this thing from me? My friend, a cat can no longer indulge in licking milk stealthily. Raja you just tell me one thing! Do you really consider me your brother?' Rakmaji asked tactfully. Raja quickly said, Bhau do you have any doubt?' Rakmaji filled Raja's glass and asked him, 'Whose wine are you drinking?' 'Ofcourse yours my brother!' Raja pronounced dramatically. Rakmaji took it as an opportunity and exposed his intention saying, 'If I can share my wine with you, why cannot you share Jaya with me?' Now gradually wine had started taking over Raja so, he did not mind. He just casually said, 'But, Rakmaji! She won't agree. No.. Not at all...' Rakmaji said to him in a convincing tone, 'If you can make her agree for you, then why can't for me? This time too, use the same strategy and in lieu of it you will get a rickshaw-ship and everyday as much wine as you want!' To this, Raja quickly agreed and told him, 'Tomorrow night, she will be with you but in the next morning I should get rickshaw-ship!' These words sent a wave of thrill through Rakmaji; he held Raja' s hand and while shaking it, said, 'deal pakki!'

Thus, the deal for overcoming unemployment, getting alcohol and fulfilling physical desire, was finalized by those two saudagars (traders) and the scapegoat was a helpless and gullible woman.

Jophle Sahib, along with his followers, was sitting in his garden while figuring out some election campaign strategies. When Devya saw him busy in the meeting, he stood afar from the garden at the gate waiting for the meeting to conclude. Approximately, after an hour when all the people dispersed, Devya went and joining his hand, respectfully bowed before Jophle Sahib. Jophle Sahib was sitting on a royal chair. When he saw Devya he said, "Hmm.. Tell me Devya, what did you bring here? Any police case on your wine shed?" Devya, politely but briskly, articulated, "No... Sahib not at all! Is there any policeman who can venture to disobey your words? Just I have come to tell you that the last week Praful Kamble visited Sathe Nagar to appeal people for votes. And, the worst thing for you is, the referendum of Sathe Nagar is entirely careening towards him." Jophle Sahib laughed villainously and asked one of the men to call Rakmaji. As soon as Rakmaji received the message, he reached at the Amdar Niwas (the bungalow of MLA) and stood in front of Sahib lowering his head down like a slave and uttered a typical slavery expression, "Sahib, any hukkum (order) for me." Jophle Sahib, with frowned face, ironically said, "Hum.. Honourable Member of Municipal, Rakmaji! Do you know what is happening in your ward?" Jophle Sahib paused for his answer but after looking at his bewildered and terrified face, Jophle Sahib laughed mischievously and sarcastically said, 'leave it now!' Then he dramatically changed his tone and sternly ordered him, "The election is tomorrow, so tonight purchase the voters; give two thousand rupees to each and for getting the confirmation of their votes in our bag, use the last year's strategy." Devya exclaimed, "Sahib, it is a very big amount!" To this, Sahib laughed and said triumphantly, "This is the smallest investment. You won't understand!" He then beckoned to one of the men and in no time, the man fetched two bags and handed over them to Rakmaji.

In the evening Devya and Rakmaji intimated all the people to assemble at Mitramamdal Katta. After sometime there was a huge crowd at Mitramandal Katta. Standing in groups, people were inferring and interrogating each other the reason of the sudden call. "Everybody, look here" with this announcement, Devya attracted people's attention towards Mitramandal Katta on which Rakmaji, Sanjya and Devya himself were standing. Then, Rakmaji Bhau came forward and said, "Look my dear ones, for the last twenty years we have been loyal to our dear and generous leader, Jhople Sahib. This year also we shall continue our loyalty towards him by electing him as our MLA once again. So, everyone please say after me." Before shouting slogans, he cleared his throat and shouted, "We shall vote for one and only Jophle Sahib." However, only few people followed and the rest showed their unwillingness through their silence. This made Rakmaji angry and partially stunned but at that moment, he subjugated his impulse. Then, in a serious tone he pronounced, "Jophle Sahib has offered a thousand rupee each to the ones who will vote for him. So, those who are willing to vote for him can collect their amount right now from here and unwilling ones can vacate the ground please. Tomorrow, Praful Kamblya is going to pay you 2,000 each, I mean to say 2,000 dry words; with that you can buy your monthly ration or something else." Now, slowly everyone started standing in the line to sell their precious right to vote. Some of the groups whispered, "Who is going to see whom we have voted? We will take the money, but vote for Kamble Sahib. Let's take the money. It will arrange at least ten days' ration."

But Rakmaji Bhau was a step ahead, he asked Sanjya to fetch a Pardi of Yeda Aie, (a round sacred basket made up of cane to receive alms in the name of the Goddess Yeda Aie). Soon the Pardi was arranged. When people in the line saw the Pardi, they looked tense and apprehensive. Now, they found themselves in a great dilemma. Before paying money, Rakmaji Bhau was asking everyone to place his / her hand on the sacred Pardi and repeat after him, "On the oath of Yedaie, I promise that I shall vote only for Jophle Sahib." Thus, by exploiting superstition as an infallible weapon and luring commoners with bribery, these shrewd puppets in a corrupted politician's hand, lumbered their demand upon the superstitious destitutes of Sathe Nagar. Even in the distribution of bribery, there was corruption.

Few days after the election, Rakmaji Bhau called Raja at Devya's wine-shed, handed him a key of rickshaw and told Devya, "Henceforth, everyday give him as much wine as he wishes to drink. Ok?" Devya nodded his head perhaps with a question in his mind, Why? Then, Rakmaji turned to Raja and asked, "Then bring the hen tonight at Sanjya's home." To this, Devya laughed and said, "That is a perfect rendezvous for this work, otherwise, Sanjya has no use of that room; he lives more in or beside a gutter than at the room!" On this, all of them laughed and sat to drink and after an hour Raja and Rakmaji dispersed.

Now it was 1 am, Nagar had fallen in a deep slumber; roads were empty, houses were dumb, whistling of nocturnal insects and a distant barking of a dog were sounding mysteriously. Jaya had slept in the house yard beside her children. Raja quietly moved her arm so as to wake her up. As she opened her eyes, she saw the face she disliked the most but without any word she opened the door noiselessly and went inside the home. Raja too followed her, closed the door, sat on the cot with a fake frowned face for a minute and said, "Now, I don't think that your conjugal life will survive anymore!" Jaya angrily but slowly shouted at him, "You son of bitch, don't speak inauspiciously. I will never let that happen! And now stop coming here; it is enough now."

Raja mischievously laughed and said, "I will stop no doubt but how will you quieten Rakmaji Bhau." To this, Jaya was stunned and asked him what he meant. Raja told her that Rakmaji Bhau had come to know about their affair and the next day he would go to Katwadi to inform about it to her in-laws. Listening to him, Jaya behaved like a consummate one; while crying, she pulled her own hair, scratched on her face and eventually she clenched his throat like a mouse biting a snake saying, "You Satan! You have devastated my children's and my life...! I won't leave you!" Raja angrily and forcefully slapped in her face and by the thrust of the slap Jaya fell aside. He stood up and said, "Now see what I do. Rakmaji is going to reveal this matter tomorrow but I will wake up your children and neighbours and will reveal the matter now." To do so, as he moved towards the door, frightened Jaya quickly embraced his legs so as to dissuade him from doing that. She kept on pleading him but he went on moving and dragging her. "Whatever you say, I will do it but for God's sake stop it now. In the morning I will approach Rakmaji Bhau and will beg for his mercy!" these words of Jaya stopped him. Then, he told her that if she wanted to continue with her married life, she would have to go with him to Sanjya's house right away. When she asked "For what?", he told her that that night Rakmaji Bhau had stayed at Sanjya's house. So, she would have to go with him there to convince him. Initially, Jaya hesitated to do so by telling him that her children were alone but eventually she had to agree.

Jaya wrapped a blanket around herself from head to knee except eyes and in that dead silence of night they set off to Sanjya's house. Raja was 12-15 metre ahead of her. She, being frightened and full of thoughts, was following him. The middle passage in between lanes of houses was a little dark, so Jaya was walking stealthily and carefully. In between, she felt someone was chasing her; so she turned back again and again to ensure if there was someone behind her. Suddenly she stepped on an unstable slab of stone, which banged down and reverberated the ambience. It alerted the nearby stray dogs and in the next moment a pack of ferocious dogs, with intensive barking, paced towards the lady wrapped in the blanket. When she saw the dogs coming towards her, for a moment, she went blank but later inadvertently ran towards the Smashan Bhoomi (grave yard) in the pitch blind darkness in order to protect herself from the uncouth and fearsome dogs. Suddenly, someone saw the chase and shouted loudly, "Thief... Thief... Thief..." Soon entire Sathe Nagar woke up and groups of men ran towards Smashan Bhoomi with sticks and torches in their hands.

In the darkness, simply sounds of breaths, running footsteps and the barking of exasperated dogs were resounding. While running when she was stepping on a bunch of long thorns or stumbling over a stone or a thorny bush, she was moaning out of agony. After a while, she could no longer maintain pace with the dogs and one of the dogs jumped upon her and with the push of the jump Jaya stumbled and collapsed on the ground. As soon as she fell down, the dog opened its jaw wide and held her calf tightly in it. It thrusted its teeth in the flesh deeply and then jerked its neck forcefully, which brought hell like pains to Jaya. Agonized Jaya moaned and noisily tried to erect but the dogs altogether pounced upon her. In the darkness, they had become awfully furious. Jaya's condition was like a rabbit, caught in the clench of hungry wild dogs. Lying on the ground, she was pushing, kicking, shouting, screaming and moaning with every nasty bite by the dogs. The dogs, licking blood on their muzzles, were producing hurly burly bark and attacking her again and again. One of the dogs was continuously trying to catch her throat but every time she was drawing it away and protecting herself from the dangerous attack.

When the dogs noticed the approaching mob with light focuses in their hands, they fled. Jaya was in a deteriorated condition, lying on the ground uttering painful commotions. There were many wounds on her body and blood was oozing out of them. Her sari and blanket were torn into shreds that appeared as if a pile of rags on and around her. When people saw her pathetic condition, they quickly hospitalized her and called her in-laws.

On the second day her husband, Vikas arrived. When she saw him and her children, her feeling of pity and fear blasted; tears ran down her eyes and the throat chocked with cry. Seeing their mother sobbing, children also started crying. Despite the injuries, Jaya embraced her children and sobbed bitterly. Vikas put his hand on her shoulder and asked her not to cry.

That day the election results were going to be announced, everyone especially Jhople Sahib, Khaut Sahib, Praful Kamble and their supporters were quite tensed. Everywhere: beside roads, in tea stalls, saloons, and at every corner of the city, groups of people were seen curiously waiting and talking about the election results. However, being beneficiaries of the day, flower-sellers were busy in making garlands and bouquets; at sweet marts, vendors were engaged in making Ladoos, Pedhas and Barfis; the Aatars had displayed sacks of Gulal (pink powder used to throw about procession) in their shops; firework shops were ready with varieties of fancy crackers and last but not the least i.e. wine shops and sheds were completely prepared with a stock of a month for the day.

Above all the substances, wine was the only substance, which was applicable to the winners as well as to the losers, because without any discrimination it helps winners in celebrating their victory and losers in mourning over their failure. Under any circumstance, the day was a pragmatic reason for all sorts of drinkers. Soon the result was declared and unfortunately, once again the ball was in Jhople Sahib's court. He had won by 200 votes. Everywhere crackers were echoing in the skies, his supporters in different alleys were celebrating the victory by drinking, dancing on extremely high volumed sound and taking bike rallies with noisy slogans. Roads appeared crowded as people were rushing to Amdar Nivas to congratulate him. Outside of the MLA's house people had gathered in a large scale awaiting for him outside the closed gate of his house.

Soon band parties of musicians, DJ sounds, Dhol-Tashas, a Baggi (chariot) were arranged at the gate. As soon as Jhople Sahib came out, all the musical instruments, crackers and slogans commenced together. This cocktail of sounds made an irritable noise. Nevertheless, people rushed to garland him but he accepted only few and sat in the chariot in a royal manner. As the procession was moving, more and more people were joining and it was becoming larger and larger. The road was completely packed. People were dancing, throwing about Gulal lavishly, drinking, shouting joyously and Jhople Sahib, with his two fingers, was showing the mark of victory triumphantly.

Next day Jhople Sahib called his most active and close supporters and told them that as they had done a lot during the election campaign, they might be tired. So he asked them to go to the place they liked and enjoy a week there.

There were total eight people in the group and one of them was Rakmaji. The group decided to go to Goa and in the evening, with a huge amount, they set off to Goa by a couple of cars. Soon they reached Goa, there they booked rooms in a luxurious hotel. As they had time, money and freedom to enjoy, everyday they visited a glamorous pub or a bar, ate different types of sea foods, consumed costly liquor day and night, spent time on beautiful sea beaches and every night spent with a new prostitute.

After five days, Jaya was discharged from the hospital. Whatever Vikas had earned during the last three months, about 95 percent of it had to be paid as the medical bill. He had earned this money by living away from his family, passing a day with three cups of tea and one time meal, selling toys by roaming on his feet in distant areas from morning to evening, travelling from place to place, sleeping in a public hall or at a railway station.

While handing this earning to a cashier of the hospital, his eyes were full of tears. When Jaya saw tears in her husband's eyes, she was extremely agonized as if his tears were tearing her heart.

Since last week, there was an intermittent rotten smell in the air at Sathe Nagar, especially Anjana, Altaf, Kaveri Nani, Jotiram Kaka and their families were suffering more from this smell. One evening Altaf found that one of the goats was missing, so he started looking for it at every possible place. In the backside of Altaf's house, there was Nava's house which was a little aloof from the other four houses besides it was facing a field of jowar and not the neighbours. Thinking the goat might have gone in the crop, Altaf moved towards the crop. The closer he approached the worse smell he sensed. He suspected that there was something wrong in the crop. He thought perhaps dogs might have killed the goat somewhere in the crop and in order to determine the direction of the smell he halted near the house. He glanced over the wide stretch of tall green crop. It was standing silently under the sunless sky in twilight. Unfortunately, he could make out nothing; disappointingly he switched his eye-span towards the home-way and whispered himself, "Finished, these dogs finished my Harni!" And, with dropped shoulders he walked his way. When he reached home, for a moment he could not believe his eyes; he articulated, "Is it Harni? She is alive!" "Yes it is your Harni and it is absolutely alive! Jotiba Aanna found it in Bhaji Mandai (vegetable market)," his mother told him joyously. But, he seemed less happy and more apprehensive. He murmured to himself, "Then, what does it smell in the crop? Certainly there is something wrong in it!"

Next day in the morning, he went to Jotiba Aanna's home and told him that the root of the rotten smell was somewhere inside the crop. Jotiba Aanna asked him what it was, but Altaf told him that even he did not know that. Afterwards, they decided to find it out and went to the field. Near the field it was stinking intensively, therefore, they tied pieces of clothes against their noses to avoid the smell. They also wore gum boots and knee long clothes made of sacks and holding long sticks in their hands they entered the crop. It was like a dense forest and as they went in different directions, except noises made by their movements, they could not see each other. When Altaf reached at the middle, he felt as if he was in an enormous green body of water but by holding his courage on he continued his search.

After an hour, both of them came out. As they did not find anything inside, they looked at each other disappointingly, unwrapped their noses and moved toward their houses. While passing by Nava's house, Jotiba Aanna stopped, looked at the house and moved towards the door. Altaf also followed him. The door of the house was simply closed from inside. They looked at each other and pushed the door forcefully. As soon as the door was opened, a chocked gust of the strong offensive smell emitted swiftly and an enormous swarm of unusual flies flew out of the house with buzzing sound. Due to the irritating smell they went little bit away from the door. They tied clothes against their mouths and noses and entered the house. In the house, innumerable flies were flying, inside the door there were several rat-holes and beside every hole there was a big heap of soil. Onto the door, the ceiling and onto walls, everywhere cobwebs were hanging. The house was divided Into two halves by a half wall. As they found nothing in the first compartment, Altaf peeped into the second one and swiftly he turned his face back. He had seen something disgusting and horrible. Then Jotiba Aanna ventured and stepped ahead to see it properly. It was Nava's rotten dead body. His mouth without lips was left wide open in which flies and worms were moving to and fro, eye-sockets were looking like two holes in the face, cheek-bones, forehead and nose were opened. The worms inside the body were crawling out of the nose, ears, eyes and around the body. Besides, the flies had covered the entire body.

Soon people gathered there. Somehow, Badal, Jotiba Aanna and Chandya brought the body out of the house and kept in the house yard. It looked very hideous and horrible. Moreover, it was so stinking that people denied touching it or carrying the pyre to Smashan Bhoomi. Thereafter, Badal asked everyone to contribute hundred rupees for arranging fire-wood, kerosene and a hand cart for carrying the dead body to the crematorium. People agreed with him. Soon things were arranged; Badal kept the dead body on the cart and carried it to Smashan Bhoomi. However, people muffling their noses with pieces of clothes, walked in the last ride of Nava. It seemed people were rather bothered with Nava's stinking than his death, therefore, without waiting for his mother and wife they burnt him off.

These days Jaya was living under great mental stress. "Rakmaji Bhau will tell everything to my husband and in-laws, I will be expelled from my house and separated from my children," these worries were burning her day and night. Moreover, when Rakmaji Bhau returned from Goa, her fear was doubled up.

One afternoon Jaya was hanging washed clothes on the clothe-line in her house yard. Her husband was sitting in the house near the door, making some wooden toys and her children had gone to school. From a distance, Rakmaji saw Jaya in the courtyard. He felt she was alone and taking it as an opportunity to trap her, he walked towards her. While squeezing a cloth Jaya saw Rakmaji coming towards her house. She thought he was coming to tell her husband everything. She was sure that if her husband knew that his wife had been used by another male, for the male's mistakes he would abandon her. Not only he but also his brothers, father and other relatives would also develop degradation for her. These thoughts made her extremely stressed, her heart was palpitating rapidly and face was covered with infinite dots of sweat. In the next minute, he was standing in front of her with a mischievous smile on his face. He asked her with fake politeness, "Jayabai, how do you feel now? Has your husband gone?" As she was frightened, she could speak no word, therefore she simply nodded her head to say no. Her husband had been watching him from the house. When Rakmaji noticed him, he moved towards him and said, "Oh Vikas! How are you?" Perhaps, Vikas did not like Rakmaji's approach to his wife; he simply said "All right" and returned to his work. Shamelessly Rakmaji went inside and sat beside him saying, "In fact I was on my way but I saw you and came to meet you." Vikas did not show any interest in talking to him; he remained busy in his work. "You are very fortunate, Vikas! You can't imagine how stubborn attack it was! But, by Khandoba's blessing your wife is alive," said Rakmaji.

Here Jaya was hyper tense. Inwardly she was invoking Goddess - Lakshmi Aie to dissuade Rakmaji from telling the affair. She was unable to work due to her nervousness. After a long pause Rakmaji interrogated Vikas whether he was not going to attend any fair this time. Vikas, without moving his eye-sight from his work in hand, told him the real reason that he hadn't any capital for that. "Alas..! Finished..! Brother, you cut every thread between our relations!" Rakmaji exclaimed as if he was truly hurt. Vikas kept on looking at him as if he had committed a serious crime; "What happened?" he asked Rakmaji with a confused face. "This is height now! Do you think I am grumbling for you did not ask me for a cup of tea?" Rakmaji spoke little irritatingly and paused for his response, but Vikas said nothing. Then Rakmaji said calmly, "If you have an economical problem, for what the hell I am here! For what have you been waiting here? Is your capital going to fall down from the sky? And, if you sit at home idle, how will you earn your livelihood? How will you feed your children?" with these questions he precipitated Vikas into a deep crevasse of worries. He then stood up to farewell saying "If you are going, I am anytime ready to give you capital for your business" and he left.

Since afternoon Vikas had been sitting quietly. His children were playing in the yard and Jaya was busy in cooking. "Vikas, do you have some curry for me?" this sudden question of Badal fetched Vikas back from the deep ocean of contemplation. "Jyoti gave me Bhakar (bread) but she had not yet made curry so.." Badal spoke little hesitantly. Immediately Vikas replaced his frowned face with a smiling one and said, "Then, what makes you hesitate; come inside we will dine together." This time Jaya did not protest. Badal entered the house and sat just near the door. Then Jaya called her children for dinner. In between, Badal spoke in a grumbling tone, "Salla! Even a single affluent not kicked the bucket this week!" On this Vikas laughed. Badal continued "Brother, you think whatever you want to think about me, but my happiness lies in their deaths." Vikas's son asked him, 'Why so?' 'Because, their deaths bring me income,' Badal told him directly and then changed his tone into grumbling again and sarcastically said, "Hmmu..! Otherwise, those who are destitute take births as destitute, live their lives as destitute, die as destitute and eventually they simply leave destitution after them for the people like me..." Then, Vikas asked him seriously, "Badal, why do you spend so much money on wine?" To this, with a fake laughter Badal replied, 'Brother, for whom shall I accumulate fortune?' and spoke in a subdued voice, 'More than half of my life is over, still i am alone and unmarried; in old age nobody to look after and after the death nobody to moan over my death, nobody to hold the last ritual pot and nobody to remember me!'. This bitter reality brought dead silence on everyone's face. Today Badal was not drunk; his suppressed feeling of sorrow was overflowing spontaneously. Further, he said, 'Brother, I don't drink to enjoy but I drink to fool myself and feel cool in the burning desert of my life. You know brother, when I am not drunk my sorrow kills me a hundred of times. In this whole world there is no one of mine except wine; it is my wife, my son, my brother, my sister, and everything!" Eventually he sighed and fixed his wet eyes on the floor. For a moment, once again there was silence in the house.

Then, 'Now have food' these gentle words of Jaya shattered the silence. Quickly, she took plates and with a small bowl-shaped ladle served a couple of ladles of Ukdda (fried stale hardened piece of Bhakris softened by boiling them in salted pungent water) in every plate and put them before the eaters. As children had eaten nothing in the afternoon, they were eating voraciously. Badal insisted on Jaya to dine with them but she told him that she would have after sometime. In regretful tone Vikas told Badal, 'The hospital-bill swallowed all the earning and capital, so somehow we are make doing with this. I hope you will like its taste and...' 'Brother' Badal cut Vikas's words in between and continued further, 'For poors like us there is no use of tongue; stale, leftover, gone bad, everything does. Because, when bellies are empty, tongues are never hungry; tongues are hungry only when your bellies are full. In fact, we are fortunate as we have at least something to fill in the blanks.' Jaya was simply sitting looking in void. Afterwards, Vikas asked Badal, 'Badal, what made you start drinking? I mean to say any particular reason.' Badal immediately answered, 'My anxiety! In my childhood every day, my father used to send me to buy a mug of wine for him. For many days I had been curious to know why father drank wine and how it tasted. So, one day just to know I tasted her (wine) but she trapped me and made hers forever. And brother, she is so possessive that once one is hers, she doesn't let him to be anyone's son, anyone's father, anyone's brother or anyone's husband.' Vikas nodded his head as he got his answer. Then, Ravi, holding his empty plate in his hand asked his mother for some more Ukdda. However, as there was nothing left in the container, she said to him nothing, just stared at him. It attracted everybody's attention towards them. Then, Vikas picked up his plate, emptied it in Ravi's plate and while washing his hand said 'In fact I had no appetite.' This made Badal felt guilty of being an additional eater when they themselves had not enough to eat. Therefore, every morsel was making him feel shameful.

After dinner Vikas said to Jaya, 'Tomorrow I will borrow some loan from Rakmaji and will go to Alandi to sell toys in the fair there.' To this, Badal alerted him that he should not borrow any loan from that Satan as he charged compound interest and if one failed to pay, he grabbed his/her house. But, as Vikas had no other option, he had already made up his mind, so he said nothing. Badal thanked for the food and disappeared in the darkness. Badal went to Khandoba's temple which was next to Smashan Bhoomi.

Everywhere there was darkness around the temple. In the North-East, about a half k.m. away from the temple, lights in Sathe Nagar appeared like a constellation of twinkling stars in the dark sky. Except a faint barking sound from afar, there was dead muteness. In that dark and isolated temple, Badal lit an oil lamp and kept in front of a classical ancient idol of Khandoba and Banu. Then he spread a couple of jute-sacks on the floor and lay down on them. For a long time he had been trying hard to sleep; turning and tossing from one side to another but without wine slumber was not ready to embrace him. His desire for intoxication was intensifying and making him restless. But, he had no money besides the wine-shed was closed. 'What to do? No money, no wine!' he murmured. Then as he remembered something, he suddenly stood up and walked in the darkness towards Smashan

Bhoomi. Soon he reached Smashan Bhoomi. There, a corpse was burning in the crematorium and beside it as always some dogs were wailing. They noticed his presence but did not bark at him for he was a familiar figure. He went into the hall in front of the crematorium and came out with a spike in his hand. He looked at the forest that lay little away from there in pitch darkness and taking a long burning wood from the fire he moved towards the deadly silent forest. When he entered it, he remembered people's strange experiences about the forest, especially a twelve feet man who was seen by many in the forest. His mind was completely engrossed in all these paranormal thoughts. Suddenly, he stepped on dried leaves and a flock of bats, with fluttering noise, flew past his ear. For a moment, he got stunned but then he gathered his courage and moved ahead. In the darkness, a distal banyan tree looked like a giant head with open long and matted hair on and around its face. Nevertheless, he was moving towards the tree courageously. Soon he stood before the huge and mysterious tree. The descending shoots of the tree were looking as like hanging serpents. Then, he held the burning wood down and ran his eyes on the ground; it was covered with withered brownish leaves of the tree and stalks of grass. Suddenly his eyes stopped the search and focused on a big stone near the trunk of the tree. Then, he walked towards it. While he sauntered, with every step the withered crispy leaves were crumbling under his feet and breaking the silence with 'Swiss... Swiss...' sound. When he reached there, an owl on the tree started hooting. He did not dare to look up as he felt the twelve feet man was sitting on the branch just above his head hanging his long legs down and all the time staring at him with his bloody eyes.

When he realized that fear was crawling in him, he quickly tucked the rare end of the burning wood into the ground, and removing the stone from that place, he started digging there. Every stroke of the spade was resounding in the forest. However, whenever he would pause to shovel soil out of the dig, the owl over him would rigorously hoot. Now, the pit had gone three spans deep still he could not find the object he was searching for. So, for a few minutes he sat on the stone scanning the ground near the trunk carefully. Thereafter, he stood up and once again started digging the pit vigorously. This time he seemed to be in a great hurry; he did not stop until the pit went next three spans down. After a considerable engraving, he descended in the pit and with his cupped hands started to shovel the loosened soil out of the pit. His cupped hands, in quick succession, were throwing the soil out like that of a rat. All of a sudden, while gathering soil, his right hand felt something like a cluster of threads; he clenched it in the same hand and jerked out forcefully. As soon as he pulled it out, it came in his hand with a loud cracking sound. To see it properly, he held it up in the light of the burning wood and viewed: it was a human head all over rotten and having empty eye sockets. It seemed to be a toddler's skull. It emitted a strong foul-smell. It was hanging in Badal's hand by its hair. When he turned its face towards him, he felt as if the eyeless-sockets were wrathfully looking into his face. Nevertheless, he placed it on the plane ground, moved a pointed end of the spade between its firmly pursed jaws and pressed another end of the spade down; thus the upper jaw was lifted up and the mouth was opened wide. He quickly slipped his hand into the open mouth, moved his fingers to feel something and then drew his hand out with pulpy sticky and decayed flesh; perhaps its tongue. Despite its hideous appearance and smell, he held it closer to his eyes and smashing it with his thumb, he examined it properly. Subsequently, his shrunk lips stretched into a broad smile, and eyes sparkled in the flickering light of the burning firewood. 'Here I got!' uttered he while rubbing the tiny object on his sleeve. Then, he held it on his palm and while trying to feel its weight, he speculated, 'This bead will surely weigh one gram.' This finding brought an optimistic cheerfulness on his sweaty and tired face. However, with a memory of one more thing, the cheerfulness on his face replaced with restlessness. 'Yes, there were three! Nava's wife had put three gold beads in his mouth! Then, where are the other two?' whispering to himself, he threw the decayed flesh from his hand and once again slipped his hand into the open mouth. This time his hand came out with full of oozy and rotten flesh, again he crushed it with his thumb to feel another gold bead, but except sticky substance he felt nothing in it.

Eventually, he buried the headless body and carried the head to the burning cadaver in the crematorium. He then threw that head into the burning fire believing that the other beads must be trapped somewhere in the head itself and they could be gained only after turning the head into ashes. Thereafter, he went to the hall and slept there.

With the shrill siren of a cuckoo, all the birds chirping and crowing flew out of their nests into a new brand sky of a new brand day. Caused by the crash, Badal woke up, tapped on his chest pocket to check the gold bead and smiled. He looked at the crematorium; the body along with the head had turned into a heap of ash. He quickly went there, collected all the ash in a long and wide piece of cloth and tying its knot, he went to the lake. There, with the help of a thin piece of cloth he sieved all the ash in water. But unfortunately he did not get the other gold beads, but fortunately he got a molten gold ring of 5 grams in the ash. Certainly, it was a gift by the corpse of last night. For the first time, Badal had got such a bulk of gold in the ash of a dead one. Bubbling with joy, he kissed the discovery in his hand.

Subsequently, he swiftly went to his regular jeweller to sell the gold. The jeweller measured it and handed him thirteen thousand rupees with a smiling face. Badal also reciprocated in the same manner and putting the money in his breast pocket, he started his way to his destination. Soon he reached Sathe Nagar and then straight away walked towards the wine shed. However, while walking he was seriously thinking about something; it seemed he had to make some decision. Now, the force of his addiction had dragged him up to the threshold of the wine shed but somehow he protested it and stopped at the door pondering over something. Meanwhile, a glass full of wine projected in his eyesight and then he grew more impatient; a great temptation for consuming liquor got escalated and started bouncing in him. Notwithstanding, he subjugated his temptation, turned about and walked towards Smashan Bhoomi.

That day early in the morning Vikas had gone out in search of a job. Jaya, propping her back against a wall, had sat dumb and the children around her were asking her for food but she had nothing in the house to give them. Later somehow she quietened them assuring that their father would bring something for them. This hope enabled the children to bear their hunger for some more time. They sat in the door hanging their eyes on the way and kept asking their mother only one question 'Aie! When will Aanna come?' and every time she replied, 'Now, he will be on the way.' After an hour, a distal image of the father reflected in those hopeful eyes that had been eagerly waiting for their father. Now, they started shouting and dancing joyously, 'Ye! Aanna has came... Aanna has came...!' This news made her nervous, she said to herself 'Today also no job!' The girls ran towards their father happily and embraced around his waist. He also affectionately ran his hands on their heads, kissed on their cheeks and holding them in his arms, walked towards the house. While going, one of the girls asked him anxiously, 'Aanna! Aie told us that you are going to bring some food for us! Where is that? I am very hungry!' These words pierced his heart. Moreover, after reaching home, Ravi also asked him curiously, 'Aanna, where is the bag?' Is Aie going to buy something and cook today?" Then in a complaining tone he said, 'Every day I remain half hungry! Now I want more!' Now Vikas was in a great predicament; the children kept asking for food, but he could not dare to tell them that he had not brought any food. He simply looked at his children with his wet eyes and sat next to Jaya propping his back against the wall. Both of them sat with pursed lips cursing their fate and engrossed in their worries.

After sometime, Vikas said 'I can't see my children crying for food! But, what to do? I am ready to work hard but there is no work!' Then Jaya, with her eyes fixed on the front wall, asked him, 'That day you had told me that under Rojgar Hami Yojana if you don't get an employment on a day, you will get wages for the day, hadn't you?' 'Yes' he said in the same manner. Further, she continued looking at him with hopeful eyes, 'Then, why don't you go to the municipality and ask for some money!' To this, he sighed and calmly said to her, 'Jaya! It's not a grocery shop! You know the people over there are too cunning and harsh. Besides, a government affair means conditions, dates, long procedures and wages for getting your wages.' These words suppressed her hope. 'But my children are hungry now!' she spoke in a shaky voice. For the first time he was feeling very much disgusted of himself.

Sitting in a corner of the house the girls were sobbing for food. Their faces appeared pale and stomachs flat. Jaya stood up and without saying anything went backside of the house. There, the land was crowded with grass and different types of shrubs. She rustled along barefoot, plucked plentiful some sorts of leaves hastily and by collecting them in the loose end of her sari, rushed back to her house. When children saw their mother carrying something, at once they curiously ran after her asking, 'Aie! What have you brought? Now, will you serve us something to eat?' 'Yes I have brought food for you. Now, you just go and sit aside as long as I cook it,' she told them convincingly. She quickly lit firewood in the earthen stove, put a big container on it, poured some water, added salt, mixed all leaves in it and heated the concoction for some time. Vikas was helplessly watching it and children were eagerly waiting with bowls in their hands. They looked happy as they were going to get something to eat. Soon the concoction was ready. As soon as Jaya called them, they rushed to her and all together held their bowls before her saying, 'Give me first.. Give me first!' She served a couple of ladles in each bowl. Children took it happily and despite its taste, they began to eat it greedily to surpass their hunger. 'Is Vikas at home?' someone, outside the door, asked. Vikas quickly stood up and went to see who he was. It was Badal. On Vikas's asking him to come in, he entered the house and sat just beside the door. Jaya gave him a glass of water. He drank it and asked her, 'Sister, will you not give me anything to eat today?' It created an embarrassing situation for the spouses. They remained speechless and simply stared at each other. Then Badal, with a smile, said, 'Sister, do not be upset. I know your condition very well.' Then he turned at Vikas and said, 'Brother, you are the engine of your family, so you have to be always vibrant. If you stop, your entire family has to suffer.' Saying so, he slipped his hand into his breast pocket, drew five notes of five hundred rupees, and offered them to Jaya saying, 'Sister, please take this money and buy some ration; for many days your children have been struggling with hunger.' This nobility of an infamous drunkard moved the couple. Jaya received it with eyes full of tears and gratitude. Once again he slid his hand in the pocket and drew out all the left over money and thrusting it in Vikas's hand, he said, 'Brother, take this money.' These words stunned Vikas; he said 'Such a big amount! No! I can't.' It was hard to believe that a person like Badal can be that generous. Badal told him convincingly, 'Brother, you require it more than I require. Perhaps, this money can make your children happy and help them grow and learn.' But, Vikas was not at all ready to accept the money. He said to Badal, 'I have never seen a compassionate and noble person like you! I respect you but I cannot take your wages. You better save this amount for your future requirements.' 'Brother, a drunkard can never save. If you don't take it, it will be simply wasted on wine,' said Badal. Still Vikas was not ready to accept the amount. Eventually, Badal joined his hands and requested saying, 'Please, don't hesitate brother! Take it and start your business, I don't want you and your innocent children to be the scapegoats of poverty and hunger!' Vikas held Badal's joined hands in his and then embraced him. Badal, who had been badly deprived of affection and love throughout his life, experienced great warmth of brotherly love in Vikas's arms. Vikas told him, 'Brother, within a year I will return your money, but throughout my life I will be indebted to you.'

Now, Vikas had sufficient capital for restarting his toy-selling business. At night before sleeping he told Jaya that next day early in the morning he would be leaving to Mumbai to purchase goods and then directly on his expedition. On hearing that, her face turned pale and realized that the temporary happiness had come to an end.

Early in the morning, she made Bhakris and Thecha (crushed chillies) for him to eat during his travel, and helped him to bag his things. Soon the preparation was over. The children were fast asleep. Before leaving he caressed every child affectionately. He was going on a long expedition, perhaps, next two-three months he would not see them. He looked at his wife; she was sobbing standing in a corner.

He told her that even he was feeling too hard to go away from them, he also felt to be always with them, but if he did not go, his innocent children would be the victims of hunger and he never wanted that to happen again. Subsequently, he picked his bag and telling her to take care of herself and the children, he walked out on his way.

In the faint darkness, still the alley was asleep, street lamps were on, the road was lonely and while walking on that endless and isolated road, he too was feeling lonely and strange as if he was breathing but his heart was at his home that had merged in the dark alley. Similarly, standing in the door, Jaya, with tearful eyes was looking at the only moving distant image of her man who was going away for a long period. 'At those strange places where would he live? What would he eat? When would he sleep?' these thoughts were burning her heart. His departure precipitated her into the bottomless crevasses of separation, insecurity and worry.

It was midnight, Jaya and her children had slept in the house. Suddenly, someone knocked at the door. On hearing it, she noisily woke up. She looked at the clock; it was 2 am. She was agonized thinking that the person, whom she disliked the most, had reappeared to exploit her. The door was being banged rapidly; she was frightened but lest children should wake up, she falteringly walked to the door to open it. However, before opening the door, she asked 'Who is there?' but she received no response. Then, in order to know exactly who was outside, she peeped out through a rift of the door. On the other side, there was a weighty man muffled himself in a blanket from head to knee. Watching his strange appearance, she grew suspicious about his identity. 'I am sure he is not that scoundrel, Raja. But then who is he? Why had he come at this odd time and why is he not responding to me?' Jaya thought. Now she was scared. The door was being banged. She was in a dilemma, whether the door should be opened or not. Finally, she made a decision, took a sickle in her hand and opened the door. They were face to face now. She asked him firmly, "Who are you? And why have you come here at this odd time?" But, instead of answering her, the stranger was just staring at her as if he had never seen a lady before. His being silent in such a mysterious appearance and that also in a quiet mid-night was frightening her inwardly. But without showing any sign of fear on her face, she stood there and firming her clench on the sickle, she firmly asked, "Tell me who you are and what do you want? Otherwise." She raised the sickle. "Ha...! Don't panic my honey! I am your well-wisher," the stranger said and unwrapped his face. "Devya Dada! What made you come here at this odd time?" Jaya asked him surprisingly. "My inflaming desire and a pull of fragrance," he spoke romantically. "What do you mean?" she asked angrily. Whereas, he, in a very cool manner, said to her, "I mean to say as Raja and Rakmaji Bhau do. How much do they pay? I will pay two times more than they pay for a night. Just, let me come in." Jaya reacted on it angrily and shouted at him, "Bhadkhau! (you pimp to your mother) How dare you to say so! If your desire is inflaming, dive in a body of water permanently and put it off! I am not a prostitute! I warn you to go quietly or else." Then, he looked at her angrily and left while murmuring something.

Raja's wife was in the last phase of pregnancy. That afternoon Raja took her to Renukanani, a renowned devotee of Goddess Lakshimi Aie to invoke the Goddess for a male child. Renukanani's house was full of men, women and children. In that crowd, some were haunted by ghosts, some were the victims of black magic and some had come to know the reason of a sudden decline in their business. And, Renukanani, like a professional doctor was treating them one by one.

After waiting for an hour, Raja got his turn. The spouses, joining their hands, sat before the devotee. 'Akka! This time I want a boy,' spoke Raja as if he was ordering a shopkeeper for a grocery item. Listening to him, Renukanani closed her eyes, chanted some mantras and then pursing her lips, she sank into meditation. In the house, everyone remained mute so that she would not get any disturbance in her contemplation. Suddenly, she started pronouncing some vocal sounds like 'Ahn.. Aahn.. A.. Ahn.. A," and sitting on the same place she whirled her head along with her open hair. People joined their hands saying 'The Goddess Lakshimi Aie is moving in her!' Then, refraining the vocals 'Ahn..' after every sentence, she spoke to Raja, "Balak, (child) soon there will be a son in your family. Ahn..a...ahn..a But promise me Ahn..a...ahn..a that you will devote him to me as my Potraj Ahn..a...ahn..a (a male devotee of Lakshimi Aie)," she asked loudly "Will you? Ahn..a...ahn..a" "Yes, I promise you," said he hastily. She gave him a lemon and said 'Tathas Tu' (may your wish be fulfilled) Thus, Raja took it and with his wife went back to his house.

With the sunset, people after day's painstaking jobs, started coming back to their houses. The wine sheds in the area were getting crowded and noisy. At some of the places drinkers were quarreling, exchanging extremely abusive words, blows and kicks for trivial matters. At Devya's wine shed, Raja, Sanjya and Chandya had sat indulging in consuming liquor and having a chat on a rubbish topic. In between, Devya, while pouring wine in a glass, asked Raja, mischievously, "Raja, how is Jaya?' 'Am I her husband? Go and ask this question to that scoundrel Vikya," Raja retorted. Raja's companion laughed loudly at Devya. "If Vikya were here, why would I have asked this question to you?" Devya spoke ironically. The companions burst into laughter on this retort too. Raja angrily stood up and left the wine shed.

Jaya and her children were dining, at that time, Raja peeped into the house. As soon as Jaya took his notice, she went outside apprehensively so as to keep her children away from this matter. "You son of a bitch! How many times I have told you not to come to my house in the presence of my children! Now get lost from here," Jaya expressed her anger. "Hai you Chhamak Chhallo (coquettish lady), don't flutter your sparrow-wing like tongue before this eagle, otherwise; I will cut it off your mouth, understood?" "You, eagle? Hmm! Even the vulture would die of disgust if you are given its title," with these words Jaya humiliated him, but he laughed shamelessly and said, 'I liked it. I think now you are not worried about your conjugal life that is why you have lost your control over your tongue. But, don't worry. I know how to rein an uncontrolled mare like you." Then, he told her in a serious voice, 'Tonight, I am coming, be ready' and went. She went inside the house and without finishing the food in her plate, washed her hands. She spread a carpet in the courtyard and lay on it to sleep. Children too finished their dinner and quietly slept beside her. She was fed up with this regular exploitation, so at any cost she wanted to get rid of him. Apparently, her eyes were fixed to the enormous sky and those uncountable tiny twinkling stars but inwardly she was ruminating a plan that would ensure her permanent salvation. As it was a strange and horrible one, there was strong dispute over it between her counter-minds. Ultimately, she made up her mind to carry it out. Then, she went inside the house, drew a sickle out of an iron tin and put the sickle underneath a pillow on the bed. She then went outside and once aging laid down on the mat staring at the sky. Now, her eyes were reflected with the light of gleaming stars and her mind was fully determined to crush the bug that had been sucking her blood for a long time.

Raja was yet at home. After indulging in consuming meat and liquor, he belched loudly and washed his hands in the plate. His wife gave him a matchstick and picked up his used plate. He was pondering over something while peeking his teeth. Then, he stood up and wore his chappals. While he was just about to step out the threshold, his wife, with a little apprehension asked him, "Where are you going at this late night?" He did not like it; he shouted, "You bitch! So far thousands of times I have told you that never to ask such a question, when I am going out. But, I think you won't understand orally." With these words, he left the house and now his lust set him on the way to Jaya's house. Vikas's long stay had deprived Raja of his daily meeting with Jaya. So, he was increasingly impatient to fulfill his lust. His piled up lust set a super rapid motion in his lungs. Therefore, he cut half the way in a few seconds. However, while he was advancing to his destination, suddenly someone caught him by his collar and jerked back. Due to the sudden thrush, he landed on the rough road by his buttocks. This sudden attack bewildered and terrified him. Despite pains in his heap bones, he hurriedly erected on his feet and turned to counterattack the person. However, after glancing over the face, his bewilderment was dissolved into the stream of consciousness and the reason. Then while rubbing his hipbones, though he was certain about the reason, he shrewdly asked, "What have I done wrong, Rakmaji ?" 'You scoundrel! You son of a harlot! Have you forgotten the deal? Instead of materializing your past promise, you are stealthily going to indulge in her, aren't you? How dare you to do so?" shouted Rakmaji angrily. Raja tried to explain him but Rakmaji suspended his words saying, "You treacherous liar, neither told me about Vikas's departure nor called me at Sanjya's house at night; instead you are going to her."

Finally, he asked Raja to fetch Jaya at once to Sanjya's house. Raja, without uttering any word, shook his head and moved towards his destination.

Lying on the carpet, Jaya was waiting for him. Soon she noticed a human figure at a distal sight. Initially, she was partially sure, but every advancing step of the anatomy weighed her surety to the confirmation. She inwardly said, 'Yes, he is Raja!' Now, her heart was beating heavily; the closer he approached, the higher her anxiety, fear and the burden of executing the work successfully mountained. She was trying to breathe openly, notwithstanding she felt her heart was not saturating; the temperature of her body had drastically increased. In fact, she was a light hearted, shy and a timid lady but the regular annoyance had coaxed her to take such a bold step. Finally, Raja reached there and stood by her head.

Albeit she was awakened, she closed her eyes and pretended to be asleep to hide her nervousness. He placed his hands on her shoulder and her heart leaped; it began palpitating unusually. However, somehow, she managed to suppress her stress. She casually woke up and calmly went inside the house.

He leisurely followed her. Before he could say something, she closed the door. Then, she sat on the cot and gradually started to slip her hand under the pillow. When she felt the handle of the sickle, a wave of strange thrill ran through her. In a moment, it stroke both her heart and brain together. Under the pillow, she fastened her clench on the handle and waited for him to come closer. Her rapid heartbeats were echoing in her ears, the body was shivering and emitting heat and sweat. Whenever, she felt he was moving to her, she was missing her breath in the apprehension of missing the attack. But, he was standing like a statue near the door while contemplating about something.

Finally, as he made his decision, he concluded his contemplation and said to her, "At once come with me to Sanjya's house.' 'Why' asked she normally but firmly. 'For dissuading Rakmajibhau from exposing our matter to your in-laws.' These words slackened her clinch on the sickle. He further told that since Rakmaji had been busy in the election campaign last month, he could not spare time to meet her in- laws. But, the next morning his visit to Katwadi was certain. He further added, 'Let's go Jaya, don't miss this opportunity, I am sure pleading will work.' She was utterly confused now, 'Whether to go or not to go' was like a Yakshash question for her. Besides, Raja's haste was an addition to it. He was intermittently asking her to hurry up. Finally, she decided to meet Rakmaji and beg for her family. Thus, Raja sighed and walked out and she followed him.

While walking she was feeling strange and insecure. The fear of last time's dog- attack and being found herself with a man by someone at the odd hour of the night had brimmed her with nervousness. Moreover, she was afraid of facing Rakmaji. She was inwardly praying Lakshimi Aie to help her come out of the evil-circumstances. The closer she reached the house, the faster her heart throbbed.

The door was open. Raja entered the house and beckoned to her to come inside. She was more nervous now. Somehow, with little hesitation she stepped into the house. Rakmaji, stretching his legs, had sat on the cot having a glass and a bottle of wine beside him. The moment he saw her a wave of thrill vibrated him. Simply a glance over her surfaced figure wheedled his lust; every cell of his body studded with excitement and joy. But, without showing a stress of it on his face, he deliberately asked her "What made you to be here at the late hour of the night?" In reply, she hesitantly said, "Bhau, I beg for your mercy! For God's sake, please do not tell anything to anyone about the things that you have come to know. Bhau believe me, I am not wrong, it is this scoundrel Raja who has been threatening and obligating me to do the things I dislike! Bhau, this Satan has been exploiting me under the threat of spoiling my family life an...' 'Enough!' Rakmaji shouted. He signalled Raja to come closer to him. Raja did so thinking Rakmaji wanted to tell something secretly in his ear; he gave his ear to Rakmaji and waited for his words. In the next moment, he felt a harsh bang of a heavy hand on his earlobe; he heard an intensive whistle that not only echoed in the ear but it also vibrated his entire head. For a while, he got perplexed, he could not comprehend what Rakmaji said or did, but finally when he recovered from his perplexity, his enlarged eyes, raised eyebrows and wrinkles on the forehead reflected his feelings of anger, humiliation and shock. He felt the finger marks on his cheek while staring at Rakmaji. "You son of witch! How dare you to stare at me! Leave at once or I will thrash you to death!" shouted Rakmaji. Raja, grinding his teeth noisily and clenching his fist forcefully, left the house dumbly.

Now, Rakmaji turned to Jaya. He questioned her firmly, "Did you have illicit relation with him or not?" She replied, 'He made me do so against my will.' He said to her, 'I don't know whether it was for your will or against your will, I just know that you did it and that is sufficient for me to tell your brothers in-law.' These words changed her view about him. She realized that he was also an opportunist like Raja; still she once again pleaded him to have mercy upon her and her children. Now, the chameleon had borne its real skin. He stood up and asked, "What's my profit in doing so?" "Bhau, in your comparison I stand nowhere; I am a destitute, so has nothing to offer you except showers of blessing originated from the bottom of my grateful heart," said she softly. 'Ha...! You know you are like that dupe deer, which restlessly wonders helter-skelter in search of the fragrance that comes from its musk in its own navel. I don't want your showers of blessing,' said he. Then, he changed his tone and added poetically, 'I am a thirsty lark waiting for the rainfall of love – you better fulfill my thirst with the showers of love.'

Now, she perceived his intention. She was already tired of the harassment by Raja hence she did not want to find herself in the trap of another tyrant. Therefore, she thought of scooting and for executing it, she quietly turned to the door while he bent for filling his glass with wine. But, no sooner did she step out of the house than he dropped the glass down, ran and firmly held her by her hair. She was attempting to free herself. But, he was forcefully dragged her inside by her hair and in protest, she, like a mouse under a cobra's jaws, scratched and bit on his hand, abusing, jostling and also pleading for mercy. Nevertheless, it could not affect the masculine hunger and its force that had already grown wild and impatient. Finally, with a forceful jerk, he pulled her inside and hastily closed the door. Now, the protest was dead; weakness was hunted by shrewdness, greed and power and now being paralyzed it lay helplessly.

With the arrival of morning, uncountable flocks of birds especially crows, with their harsh cawing, flew off the Smashan forest awakening the sleeping and dreaming eyes in the vicinity. Near the Mitramandal Katta, a couple of dogs were attacking each other playfully; perhaps, they would be practicing for enhancing their battling skills. Meanwhile, one of the dogs showed its disinterest in the play and started sniffing the things around. It wandered smelling the objects that came across it. Finally, its search stopped. Sanjya had been lying on the road since the previous night stretching his legs and hands in a full free style. There were also a few crows making back and forth around him. The dog sniffed his hands, head, eye and then lifted one of its hind-legs and sprinkled the warm water on his open mouthed face. "Rain... Rain of wine! Daaru is descending from heaven! Fill the pots and drums!" shouted Sanjya with close eyes and by the time he opened his eyes and perceived what was the rain of, the dog made one bound in the air. While wiping his mouth with his shirt he shouted, "You son of a bitch! I will not spare you; I will thrash you to death!" Then, he stood up and walked directly towards the wine- shed.

Yet, Devya's Daru Adda was not opened, in the yard of this Adda many comrades, while rubbing their eyes and yawning, had been waiting for Devya restlessly. Someone carrying a bucket of water in his hand approached the comrades asking 'yet not opened?' Reeshya responded to him saying, 'No, by then go and empty your belly.' Someya regretfully said to Kishiya, 'Ha teri ki ! That is the problem; until I have at least a mug of wine in the tummy and a couple of pinches of tobacco in the mouth, the belly doesn't get emptied.' Soon Devya came with a drum containing 20 liters of wine. While opening the door he clearly warned the customers that those who had no hard cash must not huddle in and around the shed. 'Don't worry Devya, nobody has come without money; just open it quickly. Otherwise, if my wife finds me here, she will certainly make me cashless,' said one of the comrades to Devya. Devya placed the drum, mugs and glasses in a proper order, applied kumkum to them, offered some flowers, chanted some mantras and then began to serve wine to the customers. Some of the men gulped wine quickly and left the place but the indifferent ones sat there enjoying wine sip by sip. Soon Sanjya arrived there still abusing the dog. As he had no money, he sat outside Adda begging every visitor for a glass of wine. However, nobody entertained him.

Now in the east, the golden hemisphere was gradually rising and illumining the day. The folks, carrying buckets of water in their hands, were walking hot foot on the way to Hagandari. However, on the way many men were first stationing at Adda for a while and then proceeding to their destination. Yet, nobody had bestowed mercy upon Sanjya. Nevertheless, without demoralizing his unyielding optimistic spirit he had been sitting there. 'Hey Bagad billa! Have you got the uttara (wine) or not?' these words of his mate, Chandya brought a pleasant smile on Sanjya's face. Now, he got assurance of getting something. He sadly replied, 'No battya (the informal way of addressing man). Not a single son of bitch offered me even a half glass of wine.' 'Yes, you deserve it. You work like a yoked bull and spend wages on offering wine to those Bhadkhau (scoundrel) Someya and Kishya, don't you?" Chandya shouted on Sanjya. Sanjya remained quite like a punished pupil. Then, Chandya fetched a mug of wine and two empty glasses, sat beside him and filling a glass with wine, ironically said to Sanjya, 'Your majesty dhosa atta (have it now).'

Sanjya quickly picked up the glass flattering, 'Surely, I must have done some spiritual and meritable deed in the previous birth so that I have been rewarded with a true friend in this birth.' To this Chandya said, "No bootlicking, no sycophancy, finish it quickly; another is ready.' Before drinking Sanjya took a little wine in his cupped hand and wiped his face with it. Next, he took a mouthful sip, rinsed his teeth and after gurgling he swallowed it. Afterwards, he dipped his one of the fingers in the wine and sprinkled a drop of wine while chanting the name of his late father and his recently died friend, Nava. 'Simply a drop of wine for such drunkards' ghosts?' asked Chandya dramatically for making his fun.

To this, both of them laughed. Sanjya had consumed just half of the glass; just then, he remembered to tell something. He said, 'You know Chandya, last night I dreamt of the heaven!' 'Let me know what it was' asked Chandya. 'Then listen' Sanjya said and started, "I was going to Gadegav to meet my Aie (mother) on foot. The road was entirely deserted. The wind was howling all along. In the sky, clouds had covered the sun, hence the afternoon seemed to be a dusk. Suddenly, a lightning flashed and then the sky resounded with a shrill thunder. I thought it would soon rain and so ran miles and miles non-stop. Soon I reached an isolated and unknown land. As I was fatigued, I sat under a nearby tree. An ambivalent feeling of hunger, thirst and prominently the desire of drinking darru had made me restless. Suddenly, a gust of wind blew with a roar and a mutton kebab as big as a mango fell infront of me. I quickly seized it and had a bite; I swear, Chandya it was so delectable that until my death its taste will remain on my tongue!' 'Bhadkhau, not spared one for me, ate it alone, didn't you?' spoke Chandya ironically while suppressing his laughter. 'First, listen to what happened next,' added Sanjya then gulped the last sip in his glass and resumed his narration. He further added, 'While eating the kebab, I causally looked up just to know from where it fell and I was simply stunned by what I saw! Chandya believe me, I tell on your oath; the tree was studded with crispy kebabs. A thousand of bunches were just above my head only at a han- distance. And in the area it was not only one such tree, there were several other trees like the tree of chicken lolly- pop, bushes of tandoori, Bheja fry cabbage, jojoba trees bent with the weight of fried meat jojobas, climbers studded with fried pomphrets.' He then wiped the string of saliva that was hanging off his mouth and gulping the wine in his glass, he excitedly continued, 'Seeing everything around, i got crazy. Every item I ate until I got fed up of it. Then suddenly a lightning wriggled in the sky and with a thunder, infinite streams of wine descended - pure like liquid- fire. For a while, I did not feel my heart. I breathed in; simply the gale that carried its aroma filled me with the trance of a hundred glasses of daaru. In that rain I sang like a crazy cuckoo, danced like a happy peacock and then like a thirsty lark i slowly opened my mouth and held it towards the sky; in no time a thousand of drops I gulped in a sip. What a flavour; what a divine taste; what a delight; what a real trance that daaru had! I tell you, the mirth of entire cosmos was squeezed in its single drop. I drank until my belly was filled up to the throat. It was raining heavily; I was vertically drenched. Like rainwater the wine was flowing all over the land; it was gushing through multiple channels and brooks. Several small and big ponds were brimmed with daaru. You know, every night I slept in a nest of the ostrich and in the morning washed with wine, bathed with wine; ate meat-fish; drank darru; entire day just daaru!' Here, his enthusiastic tone dramatically changed into a bitter one, 'But, that son of bitch! It spoiled my dream!' Chandya, in a playful manner, asked him 'Who is that brother of yours?' 'That dog. I swear I won't leave it alive any more!' neglecting the fun, Sanjya spoke seriously. 'Okay; oh King of Wine! Now, let's find some work for earning today's wages so that we can ensure our evening wine and food."

For a long time Jaya had been sitting in a corner of her house as if she was paralyzed. Ruffled hair, unwell face, tired-wet eyes, withered lips, crumpled and improperly wrapped sari reflected her feeling of helplessness, disgust, fear and humiliation. The apprehension of getting separated from her children, husband and family had subdued her and obliged to do things that a decent woman never does. But, how long she had to suffer from this wild and disgraceful exploitation. This concern was harassing her. Besides out of disgust her soul had boycotted her for she had lost her chastity in bargain for saving her position as a mother, wife, daughter-in-law and as a daughter. This made her think of abandoning her sinful body by setting herself on fire and purge her impurities for getting salvation from her oppressed life. But, in a moment a flash of her innocent children's replicas and a thought of their plight without her floated on her conscience. Now, the obstinate attachment of a mother and vexation of a depressed lady were conflicting for being prominent. This clash put her in a predicament.

After a profound contemplation, she stood up; settled her hair and sari quickly; went outside; woke up the children; took a pitcher and went to fetch water. By the time she replenished a small barrel and a pot with water, the children finished with their baths. Soon she too finished with her bath and cloth washing. Then, she quickly made chapattis and tea and served them to the children. While they were having their breakfast, she, with wet eyes, was staring at everyone. After the breakfast, children watched their favourite cartoon-show and as soon as the siren of a textile mill blew, they rushed for taking their school bags. When they were departing, some strange feeling shook her heart. She was so agonized that her voice chocked in the throat and eyes brimmed with tears. So, she summoned Ravi and affectionately ran her hand into his face, through his hair and then she embraced him tightly suppressing the outburst of her cry. Seeing this, the two girls too ran and hugged her though they did not know any reason. She held her all three children in arms tightly and closing her eyes sobbed inwardly. 'What happened Aie? What pains?' asked Ravi in a shaken voice. However, as her throat was chocked with the suppressed cry, she did not open her mouth, but her closed eye-lids could no longer bear the flow of tears. Tears after tears were dropping on the children; every tear from their beloved mother's eyes was shooting them like an arrow right at their hearts.

Now it was afternoon; most of the men folk had gone for earning wages, loafers and vagabonds were busy in gambling at Mitramandal Katta. Shouting and quarreling of over-drunk drunkards was ducked as they were asleep. Therefore, Sathe Nagar seemed empty and dumb. Taking advantage of being alone, Jaya closed the door from inside. Now, her eyes focused on the plastic can of kerosene. She hastily went and opening the lid of it, she poured the kerosene on her head, chest and shoulders; she bathed herself with kerosene. 'No, this will be horrid! I want death but not sufferings and pains! Even, my own children will not dare to be around my dead body. No, not this way!' a part of her mind pleaded. 'But, it's better to bear these temporary pains and agonies than to tolerate regular harassment and humiliation! Moreover, I know my children love me. That is enough for me! Now, not to yield! Lit up; no purification without purgation! Let me do now, I shall do it now,' with this thought of her second conscience, she opened the matchbox and took a matchstick. Then, with stubborn mind, without listening to the pleadings of her first conscience, she drew the matchbox and the stick closer. Now, there was just an inch of distance between the stick and the box and the same between her life and the death. Now, she was ready to slide the stick on the box. The more she advanced in her action, the more and more nervous she became. Her heart was beating rapidly and whirling sensations were shooting her brain intermittently. Finally, she closed her eyes and slid the stick on the box; with this action, a shudder of horror passed through her and she missed her heartbeat. This horror made her wish to step back from such death, however, she knew that it was late since she had already slid the matchstick.

Now, she expected furious flames catching her from all sides and burning her with intense pains. But, when nothing of that kind happened, she opened her eyes and saw; she had held the matchstick upside-down. 'God, why you made me of flesh and fear!' blaming God, she peevishly threw the matchstick away and added, 'You made death too so difficult as life.'

For many days, Raja's night visits to Jaya's house were delinked by Rakmaji. Now he had taken Raja's place and it was pinching Raja. He was restless and furious but unable to do anything. That night he concluded his work at 9 pm and drove his rickshaw to Sathe Nagar. As usual, he first went to the wine Adda. As per the deal between Raja and Rakmaji for Jaya, every day Raja was consuming as much liquor as he wanted at free of cost. But, that night Devya denied to give him free wine saying, 'Now enough, Rakmaji asked me to close your charity-account. Bravo, mirth of trance can never be fulfilled with the wine given in charity. Henceforth, pay and drink.'

'Hai! Keep this words for others; now take this money and fill the mug,' Raja retorted. 'Bravo, what's the hurry! First sit conveniently and experience how the self-paid-wine tastes,' Devya too retaliated with a mischievous smile on his face. To this, the conscious drinkers laughed. Being annoyed, Raja expressed his frustration on those drinkers with slang words, 'Hai you Ayghalyano! Why are you baring your teeth?' 'We have, so we do so!' one of the drunkards replied him and again they laughed. Raja angrily shouted, 'You sons of witches! Be quite or I will cut your throat with my teeth!' In response to him the first drunkard warned, 'Yei Raja, now hold your tongue. You are a left hand of Rakmaji; it doesn't mean you have a license to abuse us.' Following him, the third drunkard asked the second fellow, 'Hey, he cuts the throat with his teeth then how can he be a hand having teeth?' Then, the second man asked, 'What is he?' 'You brainless drunkards, you better call him a barking dog in Rakmaji's left hand,' said an old drunkard. On this, all the men burst into laughter. 'You are now in the trance of wine so venturing to speak so much. Tomorrow I will tell you when you will be conscious!' Raja peevishly addressed the drinkers. 'Barking dogs seldom bite - all the qualities of a dog are fully stuffed in him,' the old drunkard teasingly said. Now, Raja angrily moved to the old drunkard and holding him by his collar, dragged him out of the Adda. There, he expressed his suppressed anger with showers of blows, kicks, slaps, elbows and slangs on the old man. The man's nose was bleeding still Raja was beating him. However, nobody intervened to save him or to stop Raja.

The wine-Addas in the vicinity were spoiling lives of the people there. By selling this slow poison and by spoiling others' families, the wine sellers in the area were running their families. They were growing and flourishing well. The ridiculous part was that the politicians like Jhople Shaheb and Khaut Shaheb were the special blessing hands for those people by the dint of whom they could run illegal wine Addas openly.

The local police would intermittently visit the Addas for collecting their stipulated installment or sometimes they would arrest wine-sellers, confiscate the cans of wine, and in the settlement they would get a hefty amount from the sellers. Thus, they would perfectly work in alliance with each other. In true sense, these Wine Addas, Gambling Clubs and Mitramandal Katta were the obstacles in the progress of Sathe Nagar. These factors were partially responsible for destroying the young ones' education too.

An adolescent brought up in an alcoholic atmosphere, what can he be curious about? Curiously or casually drunken sip in the mood of a new year celebration or a birthday celebration or in the frustration of break up or due to the failure in an exam, would precipitate him into the bottomless alcoholic-addiction. Then, what education, what career, what responsibilities and what life;

everything would merely be insignificant and irrelevant to him. This would be the case with most of the youngsters there.

LAYER -34

Children had gone to school. Jaya was alone in the house. These days, she seemed tired, weak and apprehended. As her house was on the extreme margin of Sathe Nagar, it was a little aloof from the rest of houses in the area. Therefore, unfortunately she was deprived of the intimacy of neighbourhood. In the absence of her children, the house would appear deserted. That noon, sitting on the cot, clothes, but all the while, her mind was occupied with the agonizing experiences she was undergoing in those days. She was extremely sick of Raja, and now of Rakmaji who was harassing her on the threat of spoiling her family.

In the meanwhile, a thought of her husband triggered her brain and her heart was agonized with worries for him. "Poor man! Where would he be now? For feeding us, he is burning out himself like a candle. Long walks and loud callings day and night! Where and when would his tired feet be resting? How long this struggle?" she muttered with tearful eyes. "What's up?" these sudden words sent a shudder through her. She perceived someone's presence at the door and she quickly picked her eyelids to see the speaker. It was Badal with a jute bag in his hand.

After seeing him, she was immensely relieved. While standing up for giving him water, she said, "Badal Bhau! After a long time you have come." She handed over him a glass of water while he rendered her the bag in his hand asking her to keep it inside. "But what is in this?" she asked him. "There is some jowar and dal in it. Please, accept it for your children," he requested her. On this, she spoke, "Bhau, we are already under your debt. Please, don't take so much of trouble for us." "Baye(sister), it is not a trouble at all. In fact, that drunkard Kishya was offering this 5 Kg jowar and 2 Kg dal to Devya just for seventy rupees but still Devya showed his disinterest in buying it. So, as I had some money, I bought it." Then, Jaya asked, "But, why did he sell it at so cheap price?" "For fulfilling his thirst of uttara," replied Badal. "What does it mean?" being puzzled she asked. He smiled and said, "It means for wine, understood now?" Yet, she appeared perplexed so he further added, "That Bhadkhau (parasite) Kisha is a number one loafer. His wife works as laborer like a yoked bull for feeding the three children and this free he-buffalo almost every day fights with her demanding money for wine." "Alas, it's so sad!" she exclaimed and asked, "Doesn't he work?" "Yes, he is regularly irregular to his work," he ironically replied. However, her feeling of sympathy for the poor woman and her children had inwardly disturbed her. Nevertheless, for responding Badal's flop humour, she smiled decently. Then, she patiently expressed her pinching feelings to Badal saying that she knew the fire of hunger and she knew how a mother feels if her children have to sleep without food. She further told him that every grain in the bag was the earning of a mother – solely earned for feeding her hungry children at the cost of carrying heavy containers of soil and stones on her head throughout the day under the blazing sun of May. Hence, she felt it would be sinful to feed her mouths at the cost of receiving such mother's as well as children's curse. After listening to her, for a while he pondered upon it seriously and then said to her, "You are right. For time being you keep it with you; we will return it to the lady" with these words, he left.

After that she carried the bag inside and was just hanging it to a peg on the wall, the door banged and then frictional sound of the latch onto the hook purred. It happened so briskly that by the time she turned back to view, the door was latched inwardly. After turning, she was shocked for a moment and then her eyes were enlarged out of anger. "You Naskyabhadya (rotten man)! You demon! Open the door at once; be off my house!" While abusing Raja, she approached him and solidly slapped in his face. This act provoked the beast in him. He feverishly ground his teeth and stared at her with his red eyes. Now her anger that had induced her to slap him had fled like a coward friend who flees in a stressful situation. She was frightened of his appearance and unpredictable reaction but to hide her fear she kept on speaking "You have spoiled my life! I am not a toy. Because of you, that Rakmaji is also harassing me now. Don't stare at me; be off!" Her last words added fuel to fire and he slapped her and hysterically went on slapping her rigorously on cheek, on back, on head, on chest and everywhere. He was slapping so furiously and harshly that wherever his hand banged on her body it left its finger-prints there. Every slap was agonizing and making her cry louder. But, the louder she cried the more harshly he beat. Finally, when he was exhausted, he stopped. Lying on the floor, she was miserably sobbing and moaning. Being tired, he too was breathing heavily. He moved to the shelf, took out the hanging knife and paced towards her saying, "Today, I will defile your face! You slapped me! Now you want only Rakmaji, don't you?" Seeing the frustrated man approaching her with a knife in his hand, her brain lost its control over her organs. She was terrified, her limbs were quivering; her eyes were filled with horror. This time she concentrated her entire strength in her feet and nosily sprang up on her feet. She tried to run towards the door but by the time, her hair was in his hand. Still, she frenziedly stepped towards the door pulling him after her like a cart. Then, he left her hair, tangled his left hand around her neck, and pressed her back against his chest. Now, she was frantically sliding her legs on the floor and trying to slacken the elbow fold on her throat. "Flutter like a sparrow, as much as you wish!" shouted Raja and kept her holding until she grew tired. After some moments, her forceful movements lessened and gradually slowed down. Now she was panting, crying and pleading him to leave her. "No, not at all until I cut off the peak of your nose, I won't release you at any circumstances!" he threatened her and raised the knife above her nose to strike at the top of the nose. She jerked and shook her head attempting to miss the swipe of the knife, but ultimately the knife swished and sprinkled her sari with drops of blood. Jaya shrieked agonizingly and collapsed on the floor. Due to the sudden nervousness, her jaws were locked and she lay unconscious. As Raja's anger was materialized, he ran away from there. After a few minutes ' My nose.... My nose .....!' saying so she returned to her consciousness. She felt the sliced fore-nose that hung onto her lips and burst into mounted cry. Now she wailed; pulled her hair; banged her hands on the ground and chewed her own hands wildly. Soon her mourning attracted a crowd to her house. After seeing her swinging fore-nose, everyone in the crowd was shocked. They asked one another "Who has done it? How did it happen?' and so on. From the crowd, Anjana went and stroke her head gently, tied her hair, gave a glass of water and calmed her down. She also cleaned the drops of blood on Jaya's face, neck and hands with a wet cloth. Soon Badal and Altaf arranged an auto-rickshaw and took her to the civil hospital.

After half an hour, Jaya came out of the doctor's chamber. Fortunately, the swinging part of the nose was rejoined with stitches but now the straight and elegant nose that added charm to her face appeared ridiculous. Her father-in-law, who had been living with his daughter and son-in-law, had come to the hospital to see Jaya. When she saw him, she noisily covered her head with the lose end of her sari and even though she was seriously wounded, she stood carefully with her eyes towards the ground. He asked her how it happened but she dared not to tell the truth. She told him in a lower tone that while cleaning the cob webs in the house, a knife, kept on the top of the shelf, dropped directly on her nose. Meanwhile, her sister- in-law along with her husband came. They also asked about the happening and then her sister-in-law told that she tried Vikas's mobile number but it was out of service. She also told her that Jaya's mother had been told and she would reach within an hour. Afterwards, Jaya's brother-in-law arranged a rickshaw to send her back to home. Jaya had something to ask her sister-in-law but consistence presence of her father-in-law did not give her any scope to do so. Hence, Jaya sat into the auto with immense burden of fear and worries on her depressed mind and left to her dark future.

In the evening, people returned from the work and now the wine addas were crowded with customers. At Devya's wine adda, Raja and his mates Rishya, Chandya and Sanjya were enjoying sips of wine with the talk on their favourite topic. Beside them another group of drunkards, in which Badal was also sitting, was discussing about the afternoon scene. While, slangs and curses delivered by a woman outside adda attracted everyone's presence. "You Naskyabhadya (rotten freeloader)! May God crush you to pulp under a truck! You come out at once! You Bhadkhau! For drinking this urine, you sold out the grains in the house! Now how do I fill the bellies of my four children for a week? May the curse of all worlds befall on you for depriving my children of food! I say you come out, you blood-sucker!" shouted Kishya's wife furiously. "Aar (hey) Kishya, it is your Kalkimata. I think today is your doomsday!" Sanjya teased Kishya and everyone in the adda laughed. Raja exclaimed, "I spit on your life! A husband gets abused by his wife; disgusting, shame on you!" Kishya angrily consumed glass after glass and when he tried to stand up, he bounced back by his buttocks. He collapsed as many times as he tried to erect on his feet; sometimes on a drunkard, sometimes on a mug and sometimes on his friends. He swayed backward and forward and shouted "ca....ll, call a barber, keep the graveyard ready, shave my head right now and arrange her funeral! Tomorrow, she won't be alive." Meanwhile, she entered and shouted, "You piglet! Why don't you die! Let me and my children live happily." She then caught his collar and asked, "Tell me, to whom have you sold the grains? Or I will kill you." "How many lacks... you have been given... my opponent party to blacken my reputation? Tell... Me!" Kishya shouted in unstable pitch. Seeing spouses quarreling at the wine adda, Devya shouted, "Hey Savita, you and your husband go out and make as much uproar as you want. Unnecessarily, don't shout here." Savita retorted, "Hoy....(yes), your decent drinkers are getting disturbed, aren't they? But, do you know how much trouble your wine causes to us every day and night?" "Hey Bhatakbhavane [wandering lady]! Don't talk anything nonsense about my business. From tomorrow, tie your husband to the loose end of your sari. Don't let him come here," said Devya rowdily. Savita too added, "By running this business, you are not earning money; you are earning simply sins and curses of wives and children. You won't be happy with this money in your life." Now Devya lost his temper. He pushed her outside and then caught Kishya's leg and dragged him too out of adda. Kishya's friends did or said nothing, but simply kept watching quietly.

Then, Badal immediately went outside and approaching Savita said, "Hey Savita taie [sister], your jowar and dal is safe with me." "Really, if it is true, my children would certainly bless you for returning their morsels!" she exclaimed. When Badal told her that her husband had sold the bag of jowar and dal just for seventy rupees, she banged her palm on her forehead. She further added, "It was my weekly grocery! This Satan has harassed me and my children to death. I tell you Badal, no wife should get such a rascal husband! The moment he dies, I will offer a festoon of eleven coconuts to Goddess Lakshmi Aie!" "Don't say that sister!" Badal appealed her. On this she seriously said, "These are the words of an annoyed wife and a mother – we really want to get rid of him." Sensing her plight and mood, he concluded the talk and went to fetch the bag of grain. After his departure, she also went to her house letting her husband lie beside the road.

The arrival of her mother revitalized Jaya. In her mother's presence, her worries and fear had dissolved; she was feeling quite warm and secure. Even, the kids were delighted in the company of their grandmother. They hung on her back, fought to lie on her lap, embraced her, played and sang joyfully around her. The house seemed giggling with exuberance. That night Jaya's mother herself cooked food and fed everyone affectionately with kind insistence, "take one more bhakri, just take little more kalvan." After tidying the house and washing the used utensils, she laid a carpet in the front yard and with this, the competition for sleeping beside her commenced among the grandchildren. They quarreled, cried and shouted. After the settlement, they insisted on their grandmother to tell them a nice spooky story. Watching this lovely and mirthful relationship between the grandmother and the grandchildren, Jaya forgot her pains. As per their choice grandmother started narrating a story and the children listened to it interestingly. While listening to the ghostly narrative, they clung to their grandmother and felt both scared and protected. Thus, while experiencing the thrill of ambivalent feeling of fear and security, they fell asleep huddling tightly around their grandmother.

Subsequently, finding it as a favourable time, Jaya decided to open her heart to her mother. She told her mother that her conjugal life was at stake. When mother asked her about her accident, she vomited the indigestible and ugly truth that she had been suppressing in her heart. While telling her pathetic story she could not stop her tears. The daughter's agonized words shook the mother's heart and pushed her in worries. She warned Jaya not to expose the matter to her in-laws or anyone else especially to her husband. Being in tears, Jaya pleaded her mother to take her away from those tyrants or she would die. Jaya further added that she could no longer bear the pains dumbly; she was tired of fulfilling their endless lusts and spending sleepless nights. Every moment, the fear of the men's cruelty and wild behaviour stabbed into her heart; unknown stress did not allow her to breathe freely; every now and then the flames of worries and apprehension burnt her in tranquility. The daughter's sorrow squeezed the mother's heart and made her burst into tears. In a broken tone, the mother questioned her destiny, 'Why do you serve only sorrow and pains to us every time! You snatched my only son and then husband and left me behind to live a deserted and destitute life! Isn't it enough for you?' Then, she told Jaya that she would meet those scoundrels in the morning and would request them to spare her. However, Jaya dissuaded her to do so. Jaya told her that those stone-hearted vultures couldn't spare her (Jaya) until she died or leave this house and dwell somewhere else out of their sight. The mother too agreed with Jaya's last point and suggested Jaya to stay with her at the maternal home. Jaya took it as a working solution and without losing a moment she added her 'yes', but the next moment, the expression of puzzle danced on her face. She sighed and told her mother that the children's exam would start from the day after the next, and it would last for a week. She told her mother that neither she wanted to be a scapegoat any more nor she wanted to spoil her children's education for her safety. Again, the mother and the daughter seemed worried. They were engrossed in their own thoughts. Then, suddenly the mother got something in her thought. She suggested her to hire a house in the same town and dwell their secretly until the exams would sum up. But, Jaya denied to do so for she had hardly few hundred rupees spared for the next week's ration. She told her mother that she could not pay a bulky amount of deposit. The mother and the daughter were struggling hard to solve the sum of life; to overcome the destiny. But, so far their every solution accompanied with a new sum. Perhaps, their ignorance made them to use wrong methods. Finally, the mother told her that early in the morning she would go to her home and would sell out the sewing machine and four hens for arranging the deposit and by evening, she would come back to Jaya. Now, Jaya was relieved but partly she felt sorry for her mother, as for saving Jaya's house, she had decided to sell out the means of her earning - her livelihood. Mother looked at her and as if she had read Jaya's mind, she smiled and said, "A mother's happiness lies in her children's well being. Now, my child sleep calmly; I am awake."

"Jaya, ye Jaya…. Wake up now," hearing these words, Jaya winced out of unknown terror and quickly opened her eyes; they reflected the immense terror she had undergone. "Beta! Why did you startle? It's me, your mother," the mother's image pronouncing these words halted on her eyes. It eased Jaya. "Nothing serious, just it was a nightmare," she told her mother casually. Then, the mother lit the stove in the yard and kept a tin of bath water on it for warming. While the water got heated, she massaged Jaya with coconut oil and afterwards gave her a special bath scrubbing her skin and nails gently. While bathing, the mother's affectionate touch, her care and concern titillated Jaya to giggle and behave like a nine years old lass. Indeed, these delightful moments in her mother's company had taken Jaya far away from her daily storm of apprehensive thoughts and fear. Like a possessive child, she said to her mother, "Now, you won't live anymore alone, permanently stay with me!" Mother too treated her daughter-mother like her pretty child. Then, by the time mother bathed herself, Jaya made tea and chapattis. Children were yet asleep. Soon mother finished with bath and after performing pooja, she and Jaya had tea and chapattis together, and before the sunrises, she set on her way to the destination. Now, Jaya was optimistic.

Jaya's younger daughter woke up. She, while rubbing her eyes, approached her mother and asked about her grandmother and after getting the news of her grandmother's sudden departure, she cried blowing her shrill siren. Jaya tried to persuade her not to cry but the girl was headstrong and not interested in listening to her. Now, Ravi and the other girl also woke up and they too tried to quieten her, but all was in vain. Finally, they took her out for playing Touchwood and then she somehow stopped crying.

Here, Rakmaji, on his roaring bullet, was riding towards Sanjya's house while he noticed a few workers digging a construction-foundation beside Nava's house. He immediately clenched the break of his pacing iron steed and inquired the workers for what they were digging the ground. For a while, the workers stared at each other as if each one waited for the others to answer. Eventually, one of them answered Rakmaji that the foundation was being dug for the construction of a library for students. He also further told Rakmaji that Praful Kamble was going to inaugurate the library on the occasion of Dr. B.R.Ambedkar Jayanti. "Hum... Library; and here! Ayla.., your Praful Kamblya is really an educated illiterate! Hey, somebody, tell that dupe not to waste his money," with this sarcastic remarks, he rode off to the Mitramandal Katta. There, a group of men were busy in gambling and some loafers and curious young boys had huddled around the gamblers to see their game. Soon Rakmaji reached there; everyone, even the busy gamblers bade him 'Namaskar' out of respect. Rakmaji, while reclining to the trunk of the tree at the katta, said, "Yey you all, listen, soon you will have a well constructed club for gambling." "Where Bhau?" Kishya asked. "Beside Nava's house," Rakmaji replied and further added, "Look everyone, this time, the celebration of Ambedkar Jayanti has to be an ever memorable one. Once let the people return from their work we will start collecting contribution for it."

It was approximately 11 to 11:30 pm, yet Jaya's mother had not returned. Jaya, with a frowned face and lachrymose eyes, had been restlessly staring out at the road through the door. Gradually she was losing her patience, "Why has my mother not come yet? Where would she be now? Has something happened to her?"

such questions were stirring her feeling to burst into tears. Now, it was midnight; it looked deserted outside; except shrill whistle of the nocturnal insects and irregular barking from some distal place, everywhere there was dead silence. It made her lose her hope. She closed the door and lay beside her younger girl while staring at the roof. Suddenly, she picked up a faint sound of footsteps. She thought that perhaps somebody was roaming in Sathe Nagar. "But, at this odd time in the dead silent night? Who could it be? Will it be my mother?" she murmured to herself. However, soon she realized that it was not the sound produced by a lady's footwear, but it was a coarse marching sound produced by some rough and heavy Kolhapuri chappals. Gradually, the sound was increasing; the heavy steps were roaming nowhere else but they were pacing towards her isolated house. When she realized it, a heard spooky line, "Midnight-tranquilit collapsed in the darkness is the only time for unsatisfied souls and dead ones to be up and about," triggered her consciousness. This remembrance sent a wave of fear through her. She was just undergoing this wave, another thought lashed her, and she was terrified to death. She pleaded softly, 'O my Goddess, may it be a ghost!' Now, the sound ascended and suddenly it died. She then sat up out of fear. She knew that behind the door somebody was standing. When she found some strange eyes peering at her through rifts of the door, fear in her wriggled like an eel in water. She did not venture to look at the door. She embraced her knees and sank her head between them. Then suddenly, the door was knocked. She perceived the danger and decided not to open the door. But, the person standing behind the door was stubborn; again and again it banged the door. Nevertheless, Jaya remained statue; children kept on their sleep. Now, there was no more knocking; perhaps the person had easily given up. Jaya felt the silence; slowly she emerged her head, sighted at the door and was horrified: a heavy hand had slipped in through a rift between the pans of the door and like a snake, it was moving gently on the door to feel the latch. She, instead of doing something, once again buried her head between the knees. Soon, the hand clasped the latch and started to pull out the latch out of the hook. Slowly, the latch was slipping upwards and upwards onto the hook and she was gasping out of fear. She raised her frightened eyes and once again viewed the door; within one or two more jerks the latch was about to open. The sight grilled her heart.

However, this time, although she was terrified, she hastily erected on her feet and crazily ran towards the door to prevent the hand from opening the latch. But, it was too late. Her Goddess had rejected her plea. Now, she was trembling violently seeing Rakmaji's angry appearance. "You witch! Why did you not open the door? You are trying to avoid me, aren't you? Now only morning can relieve you!" Rakmaji expressed his anger in a dramatic whispering. Then, he dragged her out by her hand and walked towards his cave, while she, like an inanimate object, trailed behind him and soon merged into the darkness.

 The next day, the morning was on the verge of death, yet Jaya had been lying on her bed. She was feeling very weak and tired. Her children, having the leftover food of the last night, had gone to school. Gradually, her condition was getting more and more deteriorated; she was vomiting, coughing and boiling with fever. Besides, her fevered brain was occupied with worries and one of them was for her mother.

At Katta, Rakmaji's work of Jayanti was in full swing. He had strictly warned his comrades not to go to work for a couple of days. Beside the road, a huge hoarding was erected. It depicted a twelve feet high image of Jophle Sahib in a stepping ahead position with black glasses on his eyes; beside him Rakmaji's image acting like communicating on his smart phone; having a huge gold chain around his neck, a gold bracelet on his wrist and a pair of stylish black glasses on his eyes. Apart from those two giant images of the giants, there were a number of small images of loafers and drunkards of the area on that poster with respectful attributes under them like for Raja 'Adhyaksh Raju Dada', for Sanjya 'Yuva Neta Sanjay Anna' and so on. Mitra Mandal Katta was covered with a colourful pandol and lines of colourful glimmering lights over it. A red colour carpet lain on the katta and the transparent yellow curtain around it looked flamboyant. Yet, there was a bulk of decoration work to be executed and so Rakmaji was hastening his men to work faster. There was a great hustle bustle of men folk at the Katta but in it, Raja was nowhere.

On the other side of Sathe Nagar, the construction of library was miraculously executed. Three well-furnished and spacious halls stood on the land triumphantly. The first one was to be a library; the second a centre for generating awareness and the third chamber was made for Vyasan Mukti Kendra. Here too, many people had huddled to know more about it.

Though the area was full of hurly-burly events, Jaya, unaware of all the happenings, was fast asleep at home. Suddenly, the door was knocked. The knock, like a rocket, entered her ear and banged. She startled awoke and sat up. 'These two demons have harassed me to death! Why are they ruining my life? Ye Goddess

Ambabai! Tell me what to do? To be or not to be!' she whispered mournfully. Once again the door was knocked. She had no other option than opening the door. So, somehow she stood up and balancing herself walked to the door. As she was feeling nervous to open the door, for a while she stood stagnant at the door, closed her eyes and opened the door. Now, the knocker was against her closed eyes. She very well knew he was Raja - she hated his face, hence she turned back without seeing his face and stood by the cot. First, second, third; one after another three minutes passed; yet the person was at the door. She found it strange so she slightly careened her side in the direction to the door and glanced over the person from the corner of her eyes. To her surprise, it was neither Raja nor Rakmaji but a stranger. The sight relieved her but "Who is he? Why is he here?" these questions bubbled up in her mind. She approached the stranger cautiously. The stranger was already perplexed and bit displeased by her odd treatment. Before she could ask something he asked her "Are you Jaya?" and after obtaining her positive answer, he threw out his dry words, "Look, last night somebody snatched a pocket of money from your mother's hand at the bus stop. Poor old woman was continuously crying!" Listening to this Jaya's eyes were filled with tears. He told Jaya that he was coming to this town so her mother, pleaded him to convey this happening to Jaya. Then, he left.

The day of Jayanti broke. There were many unusual events in the area. The paused lives were once again set into motion. People were busy in their morning routines meanwhile a man, on behalf of Praful, was approaching every door and proposing people to gather at the newly constructed library at 10 o' clock. It was a real festival for some of the decent people of the area who were aware of Dr. B. R. Ambedkar and his great contribution in bringing about change in the status of downtroddens. In the area, blue flags were fluttering over many of the houses; in the crowd of the houses, some of the well painted houses appeared like white sheep in the herd of black ones; at some places, children, in their new wearing, were triumphantly loitering; the aroma of Puran Poli and Bhaji was in the ambience. In the front yard of the new construction, a beautiful photo frame of Dr. B.R.Ambedkar was kept and against it a large number of chairs were laid for the spectators. Almost all of the chairs were occupied. Praful was cheered and impressed by the spontaneous response of the inhabitants. Before inaugurating the library and the centre, he himself led the Buddha Vandana and then he began his speech. He said, "Dear people, today is our real festival; it is a day to commemorate the messiah of downtrodden, the father of Dalits, Bharatratna Dr B.R. Ambedkar. Brothers, Dr Ambedkar profoundly believed that education is the only way to salvation and upliftment of ours. He appealed us to get educated, but unfortunately we failed to follow the noble path shown by him. Resultantly, nothing has changed; only the difference is, previously our ancestors, being untouchables, were forced to dwell at the outskirts of towns and now, we, being touchables willingly reside in the slums. Dear comrades, today we are free from the oppressive caste system but yet our children are being inherited merely poverty and ignorance. And, to a large extent, we ourselves are responsible for it. What the earlier generations did, the present generation is simply following the same; similar work, similar habits, same roof, same walls, same condition, stale Bhakri in the old plate.

There are some exceptions like Rakmaji and Devya who have

gained a lot by the means of unfair policy but in reality they stand nowhere in comparison to hard-workers like you. It is more important how you have earned than how much you have earned. It doesn't matter if you have left no property for your children, but you must educate them. Brothers, education is the lifetime and most precious asset to offer your children; no wealth except education can change their destiny and destination.

Comrades, I am sorry to say that a large bulk of population in your locality is slaved by wine, gambling and other ill- habits. Presently, these are the real enemies. Wine is a curse for us, it is a termite, which has been hollowing generations and generations of ours; it has shackled our advancement. So, unless you get rid of intoxications and ignorance, you won't be able to overcome your backwardness. Therefore, instead of building a temple or opening a public garden, I thought of establishing a Vyasanmukti Kendr and an awareness centre. Brothers, it is an endeavour to free you from this slavery and to help you live a better life. But, for that both of us have to walk half the way. I am sure together we shall accomplish our goal.' Then, he told the people that Dr Ambedkar had a great quest to learn; he was a student throughout his life, hence observing that day as a reading one would be a true accolade to him. After the inauguration, half of the gathering dispersed and the remaining ones sat reading in the library so as to pay their tributes.

At Katta, loudspeaker was shouting vociferously; volunteers were busy in arranging the procession; waifs and strays had huddled around Katta; children's fighting and their hue and cry for grabbing places on the procession-truck were at the climax; people were curiously staring at a huge wall of giant sound boxes loaded on a truck; a group of vagabonds was profligately riding on the bikes giving off the rough firing din and mixing dust and smoke into the air.

Soon after the large photo frame of Dr Ambedkar was placed on the decorated truck, a generator barked and the batch of giant sounds all together emitted intense thundering remix music and with that, excited chaps and children, whistling and howling, hurled themselves into the arena of dance. In no time, the trance of music took over them. On the beats of music, people were eccentrically rocking, hopping and shouting. The waves of enthusiasm were overflowing; the entire Sathe Nagar was vibrated by the hullabaloo of the procession. It was planned to take the procession all the way through the town. It was a titanic multitude of people moving leisurely like an elephant and choking the roads. It was proceeding from one area to another and an hour to hours. Slowly, the energetic dancing movements of the people were growing dead beats; the bubbling spirits were tired and so the enthusiasm of the convoy was declining. Music was in its full swing but the people, resting their hands on their waists, were dragging their legs nonchalantly as if they were walking in a funeral-ride.

When the procession reached the market-yard, Rakmaji whispered something in Chandya's ear and Chandya extended Rakmaji's words to the other volunteers. One by one people went decently to the rear of the procession-truck and while returning, they were stumbling, falling, bouncing and shouting vigorously. Once again the procession was rejuvenated; people were crazily shouting, screaming, whistling and rocking irrelevantly to the music. In the alcoholic trance, many of them, hurling their shirts, pants and chappals in the air, were dancing oddly. The hurled cloths were dropping down here and there on and beside the road; some of them were ridiculously hanging onto electricity wires. It was disgusting to see men dancing merely in innerwears. Spectators were sneering at them; turning their noses up at them and abusing them with the words like 'vagabonds', 'slummy-drunkards', 'crazy people' and so on. The procession of such a great person had turned into a noisy crowd of drunkards. It was moving ahead leaving back the over-drunk inebriates on and around the road lying languorously like washed-clothes spread by a child for drying.

Then, the procession entered Khaut Nagar, the zone of Jhophle Sahib's real political rival, Khaut Sahib. Both sides of the road were packed by the people of Khaut Nagar to view the procession. Rakmaji, being a staunch supporter of Jhople Sahib, was swollen with the great spirit of rivalry; he asked to raise the volume of the music and shouted 'Rock Comrades rock! Show the strength of Sathe Nagar! No challenge to Jophle Sahib! Rock my rockers rock..!' Rakmaji's call injected his men with undying force and the feeling of rivalry. For the sake of their leader's reputation, even the tired old men, abandoning their exhaustion, were bouncing like young chaps and walking by inflating their curved chests and enlarging their eyes with haughtiness. Once more, the procession became young. The excited shoutings and whistling of men and tremendous sound of the music resounded in the hearers' ears; utensils on the shelves in the close by houses vibrated and fell down with irritating banging noise. The mob of dancers had grown so crazy that the road and the walls of houses beside it quaked by the enthusiastic rocking and jumping of their haunted feet. Rakmaji, standing beside the photo-frame of Dr B.R. Ambedkar on the truck, was continuously shouting 'Jhople Sahib, one man army..! Jhople Sahib, the only king of Tarsi..!' It seemed, just for namesake it was the procession of Dr Ambedka but in reality it was a rally for demonstrating backing power of Jophle Sahib to his competitors.

The procession was gradually moving in the same zeal and mayhem. Subsequently, when the procession reached Khaut's office, Rakmaji beckoned to the truck driver to halt the vehicle there. Khaut Sahib and his party-workers were engaged in a meeting but on hearing the chaos, all of them came out of the office to check what it was. Being indifferent to any evil-circumstance, Rakmaji had been in a sort of mischievous mood; in a way, his provocative shouting and his men's uproar were teasing the dwellers of Khaut Nagar. But miraculously enough, as soon as Rakmaji saw Khaut and his men in the yard, he asked the music-system-operator to switch off the system and shouted his men to stop their rubbish. Thus, the thundering sounds were dead; the irritating whistling and screamings were quiet and a long tension and buzz in the atmosphere was replaced with calmness. What a relief it was for the infuriated ears and throbbing heads! It seemed as if after the devastating cyclone and incessant torrential rain; such a blissful and cheering silence had once again been restored in the surrounding. People in the procession were puzzled. Now, there was whispering and murmuring among them. Someone in the procession muttered, 'Khaut is a short-tempered bucko..! Even Jhople Sahib has felt Khaut's heavy hand on his both cheeks! Rakmaji's act is apt. Otherwise, it would be like poking a hive of the giant honey bees with our own fingers, wouldn't it be?' Another voice responded to the comment with hot words, 'Hye, Jhople Sahib would be afraid of him, we are not! We are also made up of flesh and blood and not of clay to feel Khaut's slap on our cheeks quietly! Aara, we learned this battling-battling and fighting-witing in our mother's womb itself; it's our daily job. Aare, no one can know this skill better than us and that's why Jhople

Sahib keeps Rakmaji close to him, understood?' 'But then, why Rakmaji got subdued?' raising a genuine question, a third voice participated in the chat. 'Do you not see, he is retying his turban? Perhaps, he doesn't want to create any scene on today's occasion,' answered the second speaker to the third one. Soon Rakmaji's turban was set; on his head, the erected lose end of the turban looked like a magnificent plume on the peacock's head. Once he felt it gently with his hand and pompously ran his eyes over the mob and then over the office-yard. The situation was normal; Khaut and his men had already retired to the office. Rakmaji said to his men, 'Comrades, it's time to move ahead but before moving from here, let's shake this land with our potent voices and imprint our trace in this air forever. Like the real sons of father Bhimrao, repeat the slogans after me five times. Ready?' 'Ready...' the mob roared. Nany shouted, 'Say, Jhople Sahib Jindabad.. Jhople Sahibancha Vijay Aso.!' The convoy too repeated the same and the slogan echoed in the sky especially in Khaut Sahib's ears who had aversion even for the name, 'Jhople'. It was unbearable and insulting for him to hear his enemy's slogans in his home area and that too right in front of his office. Immediately, he and his men came out angrily. Rakmaji was religiously shouting the slogans. Khaut saw it and shouted, 'Hey you Bhadkhau Rakmaji!' This fuming shout attracted everyone's attention. Rakmaji too paused and turned his enlarged eyes towards Khaut. Khaut kept on his words, 'Don't pollute the air of my area with that piglet's name! Shame on you, standing beside the sacred photo of Dr Baba Sahib Ambedkar, you are advertising the name of a corruptionist, white-thief.! Bhadkhau, is it the procession of Dr Ambedkar or of Jhople.! Go quietly to your home or else you will have to go directly to the Sarkari (civil) hospital that is too by Sarkari Ambulance.' The last dialogue of the leader cheered and coaxed the crowd of Khaut Nagar; the youngsters' triumphant howling, whistling and clapping reverberated in the surrounding and humiliated Rakmaji and his people. It provoked the people in the procession; someone shouted, 'Ye Rakmaji, what are you waiting for? Let's quieten these barking dogs!' Hearing the man's poking avowal, the crowd of Khaut Nagar turned furious; voice after voice shouted 'Hey you scoundrel, come out!', 'Came out you drunkard, come out!' 'Ye you Ayghalya, come out!' 'Come on, prove you are a man!' 'Come out, if you are the son of a single man..!' In reaction to this, a group of hot-blooded youngsters in the procession pulled swords and sticks out of a sound-box and abusing and shouting ran towards the challengers' mob. Seeing the shining swords and heavy sticks in the boys' hands, the crowd of the dwellers scattered; some of them directly reached their houses. But unfortunately, yet the great bulk of the throng had got stuck due to the narrow road. Behind them, the boys were running, swinging their swords forcefully and swiping them on legs, hands and backs of the young men only. Many people in the crowd were running by keeping their hands on their chests; the folks were pushing and trudging each other for making their way; in the rush frightened children were crying, women were screaming; people under the feet of crowd were appealing 'Don't trudge me!' 'Someone pick me up!' The entire Khaut Nagar was shaken with fear. In a minute it was turned upside and down. Finally, the boys stopped chasing and turned back.

Here, people in the procession were ready with sticks and glass-bottles. Quickly, Khaut and his supporters too took out their sticks and moved on the procession. And thus, a real battle broke. Stones, sticks, hits, cuts, blows and slaps were being exchanged callously by both the parties. The whole area was filled with violent shouting, wailing, abusing and banging. Standing beside the road, furious Khaut and some of his party workers were frantically hurling chappals after chappals on Rakmaji; some chappals were lashing him, and some were flogging the innocent children on the truck. Getting showered with the lashes of chappals and shoes, Rakmaji had grown crazy with anger, but whenever he was trying to get down the truck, either a stone or a shoe was making him restore himself at the same place. Hence, standing beside the photo-frame, he could only shout and abuse helplessly. But, down the truck around him, the battle was at its peak; men were thrashing each other with sticks; with a strike of the stick, bones were cracking and breaking with 'crap crip..' sound; with a bang, heavy glass-bottles were cracking heads like an egg's shell and springing out streams of blood through the deep cracks; stones were being hurled from an unknown side and they were breaking heads, teeth, eyes etc. without discriminating between foes and pals; the secret weapon, red chilli-powder, was burning eyes and wounds and triggering the worriers to sneeze and cough. The road was changed into an arena of battle. While Rakmaji was busy in expressing his wrath on Khaut verbally, he felt a heavy knock on his back; it was so huge that for a while his breath got stuck. Yet, in order to evade another such whack, he quickly turned back. A party-worker of Khaut, chewing his teeth, had already raised the stick for another wallop; without losing any time he forcefully swiped the stick targeting for Rakmaji's skull, but Rakmaji's agile displacement saved his skull, but instead of his head, the forcefully swiped stick heavily banged on the photo. In a flash, the photo-frame of B.R. Ambedkar broke into several shreds and scattered here and there on the road miserably. This event added fuel to the fire. The comrades of Sathe Nagar became more furious and violent. Chandya, with a stick in his hand, dexterously made his way to Khaut who was busy in coaxing his man on the truck saying, 'Thrash that Bhadkhau Rakmaji to death..! Don't leave him, strike at his legs; break them..!' Taking its advantage, Chandya tightly clenched both his fists on the stick and swung it back over his head as high as he could and then by gathering all the power of his body at his hands, swiftly and vigorously brought the stick down directly on Khaut's head. The skull cracked and a jet of blood sprang out of the cracks; dramatically enough his white eyes turned bloody; in quick succession, streams of blood rolled down through his ears and nose and in no time bathed him in red. Resultantly, Khaut collapsed. It was such a tremendous stroke that if it were a coconut instead of his head, certainly it would have cracked apart into uncountable pieces. Soon, some of the party-workers attended Khaut and moved him out of the crowd while the others, all together, knocked their sticks, bottles, stones and punches on Chandya's bones and flesh until he became unconscious and was drenched in his own blood. Though the sticks and swords had licked many people's blood by wounding them seriously, yet either of the gangs was not ready to lay down its arms. On the contrary, they were mercilessly bleeding and breaking each other's limbs for compensating and claiming a wound for a wound and blood for blood while trudging the scattered pieces of the tapestry under their ignorant feet.

Finally and fortunately, police arrived and thus the worriers of both the parties quitted and began to disperse stealthily. But only the ones, who had minor injuries, could manage to be off the scene. However, under the custody of police, the seriously injured ones were taken to a hospital.

Having manipulated by Jhople, Rakmaji reported the incident to police and news-reporters wrongly. Consequently, the next morning, the newspapers, with the inciting headlines, gave air to the communal sensations. All over the district, there was uproar;

appalling inter-communal brawls, strikes and street-jams. Moreover, at some places, furious crowds burnt buses, threw stones at crowded places like markets, railway stations etc. and broke public assets demanding for the district to be closed in protest.

Thus, using the sentiments of people as weapons, people, like Jhople and Rakmaji, for their selfish gains, brought about a social conflict which caused a lot of damage to individuals as well as public properties.

The cycle of time was consecutively revolving and along with it the flow of lives in Sathe Nagar, despite having favourable and unfavourable circumstances, was travelling ahead and ahead towards its ultimate destination via the other momentary destinations such as birth, childhood, adulthood and old age. However, in this journey of life, people like Jaya were paying extravagantly for keeping their journey on; it was not for themselves but for their beloved ones.

For a long time, Raja and Rakmaji were blackmailing and harassing Jaya beyond her death. However, being apprehensive of getting her family broken, the helpless lady was mutely serving herself to those two scoundrels day and night. She was badly trapped in their clenches. She was trying hard to get rid of those merciless men but every time circumstances obliged her to surrender her endeavours. Except her mother she didn't venture to disclose her afflictions to anyone, not even to her husband. And now, she was paying for being silent.

Although June was about to end, yet it was extremely hot; there was no sign of rain. Already there had been a great water-crisis throughout the summer. Wells and lakes were dried up, grazing lands were baked to bald and farms appeared brown. Resultantly, animals were starving, farmers were precipitated into the deep chasm of worries, the rate of vegetables, grains and pulses was drastically escalating. In addition, due to the lack of water, construction-sites, brick-furnaces and all the works pertaining to water were shut down. Consequently, the people of Sathe Nagar were badly starving. They were going through so tough time that they didn't even dare to drink water lavishly for filling their bellies so as to deceive the feeling of hunger.

That day, as usual, the furious sun was vomiting fire; it was so hot as if the sun itself had landed on the earth. People were in a great predicament; inside houses it seemed as if they were in a container set on flames for boiling with their own sweat, and outside, there lay eye-irritating burning plane with skeletons of trees in it. Fans too could emit only warm air. People and animals were literally harassed by the high temperature.

But, in the middle of the day, the brightest and blazing afternoon dramatically turned dark; the sky was densely overcast. This change in the atmosphere sent a wave of joy through people and animals. Especially, children were overflowing with joy; having no terror of the burning ground, they came out of their dwellings and galloped through the lanes of houses with their thrilled shoutings. Thus, hushed Sathe Nagar was once again alive.

The cloudy sky, the sweet calls of the cuckoo in the shady ambience, the dusty whirlings of wind and flashes of lightning followed by the shrill thunders finally descended the most awaiting and foremost need of life, 'water' in the form of cool torrential rain. And, with its arrival, the sun-baked and shrunken face of the earth, leafless starving trees and withered shrubs on their last legs, and all the animals annoyed by the shortage of water and scorching sun were relieved. By Infinite drops of the very first rain, the earth was chilled; the air was filled with the sweet fragrance of soil. In the rain, children, with their unusual noise, were dancing and hopping in puddles mirthfully.

The whole night it incessantly rained and washed every house, every road, tree and every stone in the area.

In the morning, everywhere there was drow..drow..drow croaking of frogs; the awakened eyes could experience a clean and bright world around them; water was gushing through gutters and ditches; on the roads, in the yards, beside houses everywhere there were uncountable small and big stretches of rain-water wherein children were mirthfully playing and floating their paper-boats.

Thus, for days and nights Meghraj, the God of rain, blessed the earthians with his both hands.

Soon, the moors turned into cool grassy lands and trees and shrubs were studded with leaves, flowers and fruits.

It was Vat Savitri Pornima- a Hindu festival which is based on the folklore of Sati-Savitri and her husband Satyavan. On this day, wives pray to God for the welfare and long- lives of their husbands. They worship a banyan tree so as to get the same husband for the next seven lives.

That day it was cold in the air, in the sky, clouds were plying cat and dog. However an elephantial snow-white cloud, which had covered the great part of the sun, was amazingly shining with its brilliant silver-lining. Opposite to it, a flamboyant arch of the rainbow, projecting its splendid spectrum of colours, had stood on the green foggy horizon. Under these cloudy heavens, the white temple of God Khandoba in the vast grassy- land, was tantalizing eyes. In the meadows, white cranes were patrolling around the black and white herds of buffaloes and cows, which were engrossed in grazing. Over a pond beside the temple, a large swarm of dragonflies was hovering. Similarly, swarms of locusts were bouncing on the bed of cool and green grass, and multi-coloured butterflies such as black-red, yellow, brown and white were hanging over the blue flowers and golden marigolds in the meadow. And, through this dense grassland, multitudes after multitudes of adorned ladies of Sathe Nagar, with Puja-thalis in their hands, were following a pathway to Mhale's field for worshipping a banyan tree there.

Jaya, sitting on the threshold, was looking into a void; perhaps, she was trying to understand the difficult calculations of life, while a crowd of adorned ladies came into her eyespot. For a jiffy, she was baffled by the sight with plenty of questions but when she sought the apt answer, out of misery and wonder at her blunder, she slapped her own forehead whispering, 'Aare Deva..! It's

Vatsavitri Pornima today...! How did I forget such an auspicious day?' And then, she swiftly stood up and rushed into the house for preparing Pooja Thali.

As it was a festive day, Kisha's wife, Savita was going to make Pooran Poli. Hence her children were too much excited about it. After a long time they were going to have a delicious meal. So her two small girls were happily helping their mother in her household work like cloth-washing, utensils-cleaning, sweeping etc. After finishing with cleaning work, she moved to the cooking place. The previous day, she had bought jaggary, pure ghee, Channa dal, and some other ingredients required for the feast. She enthusiastically lit up the gas-stove and asked her elder daughter to bring the big-iron-tin from the niche of the house. No sooner did she ask for the tin than the girl placed it before Savita saying 'Aaie, give me the first one, haan!' While unscrewing the ill-fit lid of the tin, Savita told her daughter with a smile, 'Sone, it's sinful to have poli before offering it to the God! So, first we wil...' startlingly she terminated her words, her smiling face turned frown, and for a while she remained open-mouthed when she opened the tin and found it empty. She thumped her forehead and exclaimed, 'Aare Deva..! That Bhadkhau(parasite) Kishya walked off with all the grocery kept in this tin..! May all evils befall on him..! May Goddess Lakshimiaie crush him to pulp under a truck! Only God knows what great sins I had performed in the previous birth for which he put a curse on me in this life in the disguise of such a scoundrel husband! May he die now; only his death can bring happiness to my life!' She hurriedly sprang up on her feet, took a sickle from the niche and stormed out towards the daaru adda murmuring, 'No, now he won't be any more...! Even the God himself can't protect him today! Day and night I burn my blood for feeding the children and this rascal scrounger earns nothing; on the contrary gambles away my earnings on wine!' Seeing her Kalikamata like appearance, people in the street were looking at her bizarrely. Even, a gang of curious loafers, hoping to have some gratis amusement, was following her rapidly.

 However, she needed not to go to daaru adda as she found him on the way itself; sitting under a tree he and his friends were enjoying wine and roasted beef. This sight fanned the flames of her suppressed anger; the waves of repugnance vibrated her brain rapidly and out of unbearable rage, she turned gloomy-grey. Like a lioness she roared, 'Hey you Naskya! (Rotten being), You son of a wench! You be there, with this sickle I will tear you vertically..!' and raising the sickle in her hand up, she madly ran towards him. Seeing the sickle in her hand, his friends asked him to run away, but Kishya's condition was such that he could not even stand on his own. Spilling out saliva of his mouth, he stuttered to his friends, 'He..y y..ou be.. coo..l, she.. ca..n't do any..thing. Yo..u go.. on.' And,   without having any apprehension, he kept on consuming liquor. In no time, she directly ran-over him, and lifted the sickle to dissect his skull, but fortunately one of his friends caught her hand and snatched the sickle from her. The lack of sickle didn't matter for her, she lifted her leg as high as she could and kicked on his arm, and thus, Kishya was stretched out on the ground. Albeit he had got a huge kick, he threatened her saying, ' He..y Savye go to h..ouse, or I will beat y..ou to death..!' To this, she, like a wounded tigress, pounced upon him and gave him blow after blow, slap after slap saying 'You Satan! Today, I will show you the way to hell! Here you, this for stealing, this for starving my children, take this for everyday's pilfering, here one more, another one!' she was wildly slapping and scratching him. She had met the expectation of the group of loafers. Apart from them, a huge number of people, especially women returning from the banyan tree, had gathered around them and they were pushing and pulling each other to see the battle. And, while seeing Savita thrashing her husband, many of the ladies were experiencing the second hand pleasure of knocking out their oppressive or drunkard husbands. However, some of the wives were so agitated by the scene that their suppressed feelings of self-pity and abhorrence for their husbands had triggered out. And, finding an apt forum and scope to release those feeling, one after another they were voluntarily disclosing their minds to each other: 'Even my husband too is Ragatchata (bloodsucker) like Kisha!' ' Taie(sister), my husband is worse than Ravan! I abhor even to utter his name!' 'Sisters, you just think how a girl of 28 years feels to live her life with a 40 year' old suspicious husband!' 'But, mine is not like yours, he is really a God for me!' 'You are really a lucky one! May your happy conjugal life live longer than the sun itself and may a five mouthed serpent sting my bone-enemy to death! You may take me as a crazy cuckoo but really only his death would open the doors to a peaceful life for me.'

Savita was not yet calmed down. Finally, some of the people in the crowd drew her away. But, as she was not yet contended, she was shouting, jostling and jerking in an attempt to free herself from the clutch of the people. The only thing she was shouting over and over was, 'Leave me, I want to see him in blood..! I won't be calm until I spill his blood!'

After having banged on the ears and head by the wife, it seemed, to some extent his trance of wine was affected. Although he was yet lying on the ground, he could at least speak normally. He disappointingly and seriously said to his friends, 'Somya my friend, you go to the graveyard and keep a pit of 5 by 3 feet ready there, Arjya and Ramya, you go to market and buy material for the funeral ceremony.' Then, in a threatening voice he commanded her, 'Hey Savye, give them money and then you run. I wish you to run like a terrified mouse that runs helter-skelter for escaping from its death, a cat. Here I get up, now you run, I say run, be afraid of me!' Somehow he sat up and placing his both hands on his knees, propped himself up, and when he was just about to stand, all of sudden a mild gust of wind blew and he collapsed on the ground again.' On this the crowd guffawed. Savita mockingly said, 'Oh! You are going to murder me! Come on! Kill me, if you are a man!' While lying by his belly he shook his head and said 'Okay! You want to die on the spot! No matter. Hey, can anybody lend me a knife for a while. I said, does anyone have a knife? Nobody has?' People were enjoying the quarrel. Then he ordered, 'Okay, someone get me the sickle lying over there. Hey you, haven't you heard what I said? You pig-headeds! Remember, you are disobeying none other than Kishor Bhau! You piglets and witches!' To this, a group of people got provoked and angrily fell upon him.

Since the crowd was doing Savita's left over work, she sighed and sarcastically said, 'Send Kishor Sahib to hell, and after ten days, kindly come along with your whole family to have a delicious feast on the 10th Day of his delightful demise!' And then, she left for home.

 After a long time, Jaya had adorned herself; green sari, combed hair, a nose ring having traditional design and red kumkum on the forehead gave her the look of a traditional house-wife. Wishing to have Vikas as her husband for every life of hers, she went to the sacrosanct banyan tree. She religiously took seven rounds around it while winding a thread around its trunk so as to invoke the holy tree to protect her husband from all evil-power and fulfil her wish.

Here, with a scowled face, Savita reached home. She hurriedly entered it and angrily banged the door shut. Then, she hastily replaced her sari with a new one, whiten her dark complexion with a thick layer of talcum powder; applied a dark red lipstick on her lips between which two long upper teeth peeped out; put on a maroon bindi on her brow; darkened her ratty eyes with Kajal; prepared Pooja Thali and walked hot foot towards the banyan tree to worship it.

While Savita was faithfully worshiping the sacred tree, Badal came breathing half and said, 'Thanks to Mareeaie! Savita, like wind I ran home to home in search of you!' 'First you calm down, and tell me what made you gallop like a crazy donkey and to follow me here!' Savita asked him in a bitter manner. As he was in a hurry, he delivered the words anxiously and hastily, 'I am afraid, after listening to me you would collapse! A gang of vagabonds has thrashed your husband severely, he is seriously wounded; at once run after me, I will show you where he is lying!' And, before finishing his last word he turned back and started running towards the place while saying all the way, 'Savita, come on, follow me! Make it fast! Don't worry; nothing will happen to your husband.' But, when he reached half the way, he peeped back and found no one behind him. For a while he got puzzled, but then he thought that the woman would have fallen down somewhere on the way, and so, again he jogged back towards Mangire's field looking here and there for her throughout the way. But, to his amazement, he found her nowhere on the way but at the same place where he had found her earlier. He was gobsmacked as she appeared calm and cool; she was leisurely taking rounds around the tree and coiling the trunk with a thread. 'Whether you are worried about your husband or not! His condition is pathetic; he has been lying there, no one is with him and you are yet here!' Badal shouted at her. She counter attacked 'Hey you drunkard! No need to bark at me, I don't care about that rubbish bloodsucker! Now go you drunkard and take care of your fellow drunkard. And next time come with some good news.' Badal, like a true worshiper of hers, ironically joined his hands and asked, 'May I know what good news Savita Mata expects now?' 'Of his death,' on the spur of the moment she replied. Her pungent words simultaneously stunned and subdued him. Then, out of the blue, he burst into hilarious laughter. She finished her last round and taunted, 'Has Masoba (God in fields) entered him or what?' and then she asked him, 'Hey! All the crows flew away, why are annoying those poor beings?' While controlling his laughter, he replied her paradoxically, 'Now I understood why drunkards like Kishya, despite consuming poisonous alcohol day and night, live long lives. Really, Savitaaie, you are great! Perhaps, Kishya would have died today, but your love for him and the power of your worship coerced this holy banyan tree to protect him from the God of death.' She was simply staring at him. He disarmingly smiled at her and continued his words, 'I think even Sati Savitri's nobility is stale before yours, because she snatched her husband, Satyvan from the clutch of God Yamdev (God of death) because he was not like your husband. He was a dutiful, industrious, and honest person. So, there is no wonder if she saved him and wished to have such an owner of good qualities as her husband for the next seven lives of hers. But, look at your nobleness; although your husband is a drunkard, escapist, freeloader and a pilfer, yet without failing, you came here to invoke the holy tree to protect him. And not only this, but one after another in this way you have coiled the thread around the tree seven times or perhaps more than that if it was miscounted for gaining the same drunkard-husband for the next seven lives. Really! What a great woman you are! In fact, you deserve to be canonized. Rather I feel instead of observing the day as Vat Savitri Pornima, it should be celebrated by your name as Vat Savita Pornima, shouldn't it be?' She retorted 'Yes, why not! In this case, you will also have to replace the name of Karvachaud with mine.' 'What is it, Devi?' he asked. She coquettishly criticized him, 'How ridiculous! You are too ignorant! Don't you watch Hindi TV serials?' Badal pretentiously replied her, 'I am a poor being, and it's not for me!' She cynically said to him, 'But, the poor being has too long tongue, hasn't he? Ok, no matter, I will teach you: see, it is a day on which womenfolk wear new saris, they adorn themselves an...' 'Ho my mother! You teach me later but now first attend your husband, come with me,' he interrupted her. 'Go to hell! Let him die! I have nothing to do with him,' she barked at him. For a while he found himself speechless, then he softly said, 'Sister, please don't be angry! But, i don't understand, if you detest him so much, why did you pray the banyan tree?' 'Because, it is a tradition; every lady does it and so i too did. Now be out of my sight!' she told him. He calmly and politely said to her, 'Sister, if I am causing you a trouble, I will go but before going let me tell you that by worshiping this sacred tree on this occasion, ignorantly you have not only increased his life span but also you have booked him as your husband for the next seven lives. So, even though you are fed up with him, neither you nor God himself can separate you from Kishya ; by hook or crook you have to live and will have to live your life with him. To this, she laughed and mockingly replied him 'Hum.. Who knows whether the hell and heaven exist or not, and even if they exist, you be worriless, I will take care of your friend!' Finally, he sighed and decided to give up his idea of convincing her. But, before leaving he solemnly said to her, 'I think you are undervaluing my words; do as you wish' and then turned his face towards his way. But this time, unexpectedly his blunt words pierced her arrogance; she took them seriously. Now, she appeared little panicky and submissive. She hesitantly asked him, 'Then, how can I amend my mistake? Badlya, do you know any Devrashi or Baba who can help me to get rid of this person?' Now, the ball was in his court, he assertively told her, 'Even God himself cannot help you in this regard but certainly I can.' She found his assertion little indigestible and strategic but she remained tight-lipped. But, he read her face and said to her, 'I haven't drunk and I am conscious of what I have said. See, the reality is, your husband is not bad, his addiction is terrible, and you don't detest him, you detest his ill-behaviour. Just, check that yourself.' For a while she pondered over the fact and then nodded her head to indicate her accord. 'Agreed? Now, do you know the reason of his addiction to wine?' he asked. She simply shook her head to show that she was ignorant to the reason he was asking for. Then, he said, 'No matter, I know Kishya since he was in diaper; i have seen his every stage of life and so I know the reason very well. I will tell it later, first let's see him.' 'No, first I want to know the reason,' said she. 'Aaga! But, he is dying there,' he exclaimed. 'Don't worry, the banyan tree will take care of him – you know it very well,' she assured him. Her mulish avowal obliged him to attend her curiosity first. He got annoyed and spoke, 'Hogwash! Now listen' for a while he paused, scratched his head and then started to narrate the event in a usual way, 'Long ago, when your husband was in his boyhood, he was so decent that even on seeing or hearing the word 'wine' he would vomit day and night at least for a week.' As Badal himself found his statement too heavy, he broke the flow of the narration so as to convince her to believe in his words saying, ' Savita, you may be taking it as an exaggeration but I swear, my words are purer than Devya's wine, I meant to say a mine – gold in the mine.' Then he resumed the narration: 'One day while meek Kishya was returning home from the work, he crossed an enchanted lemon in the street, and that night an unbelievable incident happened. He went to Devya's wine Adda, and to everyone's amazement, the boy, who disgusted daaru the most, consumed not one or two but total ten glasses of wine in quick succession. Actually, it was not he, it was a restless soul of a drunkard and yet it is present in your husband. Savita, your husband is innocent; the beast in him is a gambler. It has been making him behave badly.' She looked partially convinced. She asked him, 'Do you mean to say, if the unsatisfied soul in my husband is banished, he will not drink?' He nodded positively. 'But, how and who can do it?' she anxiously asked him. He sighed and said, 'It's risky! But, I will do it for him. Now, listen to me carefully; at any cost we have to persuade the soul to release your husband. Tonight we will offer the soul a jug of wine, some roasted meat, mutton-curry and two chapattis or Bhakaris. And, you need not to worry about it; you just keep the things ready I will carry them to the grave yard where the drunkard was buried, okay!' Her consciousness doubted his intention, but her blind-belief and hope for a positive change overpowered it and made her nod positively. After receiving her positive confirmation, he added one more instruction confidently, 'One more thing, next Sunday, for satisfying the drunkard-soul, cook two hens, bring three to four jugs of wine and invite five drunkards to your house for dinner and seek their blessings. Then you see, Kiysha will prove to be an unparallel husband in the world. And, you don't worry about managing the drunkards, I know some good drunkards. I will request them to accept the invitation for the sake of your innocent husband.' 'For how many drunkards will I have to cook?' she asked him to confirm the number again. He quickly replied, 'Just five!' Then, she calculated something with her fingers and told him, 'Badlya, call only four drunkards.' He replied seriously, 'No, we need five ones! How can you eliminate one?' She explained him, 'No, I haven't eliminated one! See, those four including you becomes five, doesn't it?' 'Ayla! You are too clever!' he attributed this sycophantic remark on her and then asked her to go with him for attending her meek husband. However, all the way he again and again reminded her about that night's offering to the drunkard-soul.

These days almost every night Rakmaji was going to Jaya's dwelling. Therefore, she, putting her heart out, had to make her children sleep in the house-yard every night.

As usual that night too Jaya had been lying along with her children in the yard. As the night was reclining towards midnight, her nervousness was escalating, because the midnight was the stipulated time for the arrival of the demon, Rakmaji. By closing her eyes and joining her hands, she was continuously invoking Goddess, Lakshimi Aie to dissuade him from coming there that night. The Goddess granted her wish. Suddenly, she perceived some noise and opened her eyes and found a manly figure at her feet. This sight crushed her heart. Thus, cursing her fate, she stood up and went inside the house for performing the imposed and disgusting duty. The man followed her, closed the door and turned his face towards her in the light. Seeing an unexpected person at the unexpected time, she yelled, 'You! What are you doing here at this time? Get out of my house at once! Already you exacerbate my afternoons, at least at night let me sleep peacefully! Raja, for God sake let me live freely for a while for myself and for my children! Please go.' 'Ayla! Every time this beauty cries, until you are reminded what I can do, you don't surrender,' saying so he went and squeezed her in his arms saying romantically, 'After such a long time I have got a chance to sleep here and you want me to miss it so easily!' With great difficulty she released the grip of his hands around her and drew herself away from him. Subsequently, he angrily held her by her hair and ruthlessly bent her down and threatened her to be quiet.

Half an hour past, now she was lying beside him like a dead body. Meanwhile, suddenly somebody knocked at the door, and with this her heart too started knocking rapidly. She quickly wrapped the cloth around her and beckoned to him to slip under the cot. She was tense with the thought, 'Who is in the opposite of the door?' Before opening the door she ship-shaped her appearance and then opened it with a great burden on her horrified heart. The moment she glanced over the person before her, a thousand of times she died of fright and shock and storms of worries in her head. Instantaneously infinite blobs of sweat trickled through her brow and body, her throat and lips were dried out and her wide open eyes reflected the terror and bewilderment in her paralyzed heart. She stood motionless at the door. 'What happened to you? And, why are the children sleeping in the open while you are inside?' her husband, Vikas inquired her seriously and suspiciously. For replying she parted her vacillating lips but fumbled for words as she went blank. Seeing his wife's odd behaviour, he too was befuddled. He stared at her with strange eyes for finding the answer on his own. His staring eyes were piercing her but she was trying to look normal. Then, she somehow coped with her impulses and said to him, 'Children insisted on me to sleep in the open. I had also been sleeping beside them but after a while, suddenly I had fever and was feeling bitterly cold, hence I went inside to sleep. And before you knocked on the door, I had a nightmare; I was so frightened that I could not even answer your questions!' Now, he sighed and while telling her that the next day he will take her to a doctor, he climbed the door-step to make his way in, but she stood in the door firmly. She snatched the bag from his hands and said to him tenderly, 'You must be tired of travelling! Now, you go and sleep beside the children! Now, I am feeling better, so after keeping it I will also come there to sleep, okay!' These warm words melted the man and he agreed. He stepped off the stair, moved to the right corner of the step, placed his chappals, and walked towards the children. But in between, as something stroke to his memory, he abruptly stopped and pondered over it. In the mean time, she came out and asked him why he was standing there. But, without answering her question, he turned around and proceeded to the door with dead seriousness on his face. Yet Raja was in the house, she couldn't understand how to dissuade her husband from entering the house. She quickly closed the door and moved against him while pleading hysterically, 'Now, let's go to sleep! In the morning you do whatever you want to do! Please, I am feeling too cold!' But now, he was not in the mood of listening to her. She, with crying face, was helplessly standing while he was rapidly approaching the door. Suddenly, he stopped at the door-step and called her. She noisily ran and stood by him. He pointed a pair of an adult's chappals and asked her, 'Whose chappals are these? Did anybody come in my absence?' Seeing the chappals, she inwardly startled and thought, 'Oh my Mother! These are of that rogue! Now, what to say?' 'Nobody, actually Badal gave the pair to you,' she spoke up thoughtlessly but swiftly and confidently. He slipped his foot in one of the chappals and eulogized them saying, 'Aarewa! They are made up of original leather. Tomorrow, i will thank him for this gift. Now, let's go to sleep.' As his last expression relieved her, she sighed.

Now, lying beside the children, she was restlessly waiting for her husband to sleep; over and over, she was stealthily glancing over him from the corner of her eyes. After a while, he began to snore. She carefully listened to him and had a fleeting look over him in order to confirm that he was asleep. Thus, finding the situation conducive, she gently stood up and sneakily walked to the door. After reaching there, she had a quick glance around her and began to unbolt the grumbling and stubborn latch softly for avoiding its shrill grunting. As it was a do-or-die situation for her, she was undoing the latch by holding her breath; she was busily moving the tight handle up and down whilst suddenly, she felt a hand on her shoulder and she was startled; she quickly twisted her neck round and found her husband standing behind her. Now once again her nervousness had escalated. 'Again are you feeling cold?' his caring inquiry freed her from brainstorming another cat and bull story. Thus, she just nodded her head in response to his question. But, it was not the end; it was just a momentary relief which was eclipsed by the thought of unexpected catastrophe. 'You don't worry about me, now rest yourself beside the children,' she asked him In order to deter him from entering the house. He said, 'Okay!' and then softly asked her, 'Jaya, I have a ravenous appetite! Actually, in the haste of returning home, I have had nothing since afternoon. Is there anything to eat?' 'No, I meant to say, there is no Kalwan (curry of vegetables)!' she swiftly told him. 'Oh! Doesn't matter, I have some chili powder in my bag, with Bhakri (bread) it will do,' said Vikas. But, to avoid an adversity, she was desperately browsing her brain for a working reason but this time her brain-ware was not supporting to her search. Finding her gravely engrossed in thoughts, he asked her if she had any problem. In reply, she disarmingly laughed for hiding her fretfulness and shook her head negatively and finally opened the door with a heavy heart.

When he entered the house, he produced wrinkles on his forehead; his eyes suspiciously searched for something, and the nose strangely whiffed the air in the house. Seeing his strange behaviour, she was inwardly horrified but by plucking up her courage, she asked him what he was looking for. In reply, he said nothing, just looked at her stubbornly and after a while, while examining something in the extreme corner of the house, said, 'I can smell a strong odour of wine. Where is it coming from?' Then, he turned his eyes towards the cot and said, 'It is somewhere from under the cot.' These words quivered her heart. Before he continued the investigation further, frightened Jaya tightened her fists for coping up with the feeling of fear, and promptly improvised and narrated another fabricated story, 'Pinki has sour-throat so I had brought a cup of wine for curing it, but she spilled out the wine on the bed.' Hearing this account, he felt embarrassed and ashamed of his suspicious deeds. Then, hastily and amorously he demanded her for food like a possessive child to its mother. She too, like a mother, asked him to sit down patiently until she served him food and moved to the cooking place. But, no sooner did she pace a step or two than she was moved by a thought, 'If he sat down, Raja would clearly float in his sight.' So, she swiftly turned back for persuading him to sit on the cot. But unfortunately, she was late; already he had sat on the floor, but fortunately he had backed the cot. This picture relieved her a bit but she was yet under tremendous pressure. However, without imprinting a trace of her stress on her face, she smiled at him and in no time brought him Kalwan of brinjal and two Bhakris(breads). He hurriedly drew the plate towards him saying, 'After such a long time, I am having my favourite Kalwan' and started eating it happily. When she sat down facing him, she was shocked to see Raja's legs just behind her husband. Moreover, as Raja was lying facing the wall, she could find no way to make him fold his legs. She was now more restless.

Similarly, under the cot Raja was lying down uncomfortably; a swarm of mosquitoes was piercing his flesh with their thorn like trunks, but finding himself at the tight corner, he was dumbly bearing with it and anxiously waiting for Vikas's departure from the house. Meanwhile, Vikas noticed something; he kept the morsel in his hand on hold and asked her surprisingly, 'You said that there is no Kalwan! From where did you produce it then?' To this, she pretentiously smiled saying, 'Actually, I forgot that I had already spared some Kalwan for you.' Her expression amazed him; he felt something wrong and so he emphatically asked her, 'Are you sure, you had kept it for me?' She thoughtlessly told him 'yes'. Then, he quickly asked 'Now tell me; how did you know that I was going to come tonight?' This time she was little perplexed, she could not make her mind what to say; she was fumbling for words. In the meantime, Raja found himself in a dramatic predicament; dust in the corner got mixed in his breath and therefore the puff of dust spread in his throat and nose. Consequently, it caused him an intensive irritation that resulted into an unavoidable feeling of sneezing and coughing. However, for avoiding them, he muffled his nose and mouth but it was in vain; his nose voluntarily exhaled the puff of dust with a loud explosion. And thus, this echoing sneeze alerted Vikas to the presence of a third person. He quickly turned around and peered under the cot and remained openmouthed and eyes widened. For a while both the men, Raja out of terror and Vikas with the feeling of being betrayed, looked into each other's eyes bewilderedly. For a while Vikas could not believe in what he was seeing; he pleaded God, 'Hey God! Let it not be reality, let it be a nightmare!' then turned his tearful and reddish eyes towards her and shouted, 'Who is he?' His furiously staring eyes stung her heart to paralyze. In another moment, he paced towards the door-corner, grabbed a crowbar from there and then walked towards her exclaiming, 'You shameless! You harlot! In my absence indulging in love making with your lover! What a disgusting mother you are! You don't deserve to be alive anymore!' In the meantime, he found Raja crawling hastily out of the cot, and he lost his temper; 'Hey you Ayghalya! Stop! You son of ten fathers! Stop.. Today's your doomsday!' while abusing and threatening, he ran towards Raja and before Raja could stand up and utter a word, frustrated Vikas wrathfully stabbed the crowbar into Raja's ribs, and a stream of blood sprang up on Vikas's shirt and face.

Raja collapsed, blood rapidly gushed forth from the hole in his chest and in no time a pool of blood spread all over the floor wherein his body lay trembling hysterically and rubbing the heels on the ground glaringly.

After few minutes, suddenly the movements of his legs stopped and eyes turned white and now Raja lay calm.

 Seeing the bloodshed she was so terrified that she felt whirling sensations in her head; her body was voluntarily collapsing but she propped against the wall and forcefully kept herself standing. Similarly, her eyelids were shutting down on their own accord and eyes were sighting hazily. In such an excruciating condition, she could see a vague replica of her husband advancing towards her in an animated way with the same crowbar in his hand. Seeing the approaching death in the disguise of her own husband, horrified Jaya attempted to run away but she could not move her legs. So she tried to call her son for help, but her throat could produce no voice.

Thus, helpless Jaya could do nothing except shedding tears through her eyes.

Soon he was in front of her, once he looked at her face and in the next moment he closed his eyes and raised the crowbar in his hands up over his head to split her head. She thought, 'Now who wil I save me if the saviour himself wants to slay me?' and surrendered herself to him.

While he was making his mind to attack her, many sweet nostalgic moments, which he had spent with her, were unrolling in his eyesight in quick succession; his sympathy and love for her had set his heart on fire in protest to the idea of killing her. He was feeling the fire in his heart for her, but unfortunately, the fire of repugnance and revenge was more intensive than his love and sympathy for her. Eventually, he took a deep breath and tightened his grip on the crowbar to cut the thread of her life, meanwhile Jaya spoke in shaky voice, 'Listen! You kill me but before I close my eyes forever, for God's sake once let me tell you why I did so against my will!' He harshly told her 'I know to protect yourself you are going to wave another fine story, aren't you? But, I don't want to send you to the hell with any unfulfilled wish of yours! Say quickly. Before dawn breaks I have to set out two dead bodies.' To this she softly replied to him, 'Listen! If you think I am going to make a story to save my life, you better kill me!' and she broke down. Then, he put down his hands and insisted on her to tell him the truth. And so, she, on an oath of her three children, told him honestly how Raja and Rakmaji obliged her to do the things against her will. After listening to her, he was overwhelmingly angry; he tightened his clench on the bar saying, 'Haramkhor Rakmaji! Now, be ready to embrace your death!' and walked hotfoot towards the door but before he could cross the threshold she softly told him, 'I feel, before the night gets over, we should move off this dead body from our house.' To this, he turned back, for a moment pondered over it and nodded yes.

Jaya quickly took out the thick cover of the mattress on the cot, pulled an old blanket out of a heap of folded quilts and cleaned the blood on the floor with the blanket. After that they wrapped the dead body in the same blanket, put it in the cover and tied the mouth of the cover with a rope.

Now, the question was where they should settle the body. So, he thought over it seriously and finally decided to burn the body in Smashan Bhoomi. Asking her to carry the can of kerosene, he picked up the pack by its upper loose end and carried it on his back. Their way to Smashan Bhoomi was right through Sathe Nagar. Moreover it was via Mitramandal Katta, therefore Jaya was inwardly apprehensive.

Shortly they set on their way. Instead of pukka road, he made his way to Sathe Nagar through dark and dense clusters of meadows. In the darkness he could hardly see anything on his way, yet with the palpitating heart under the burden of the dead body, he was rapidly marching in the direction to the distal glittering lights of Sathe Nagar while trudging grass, clusters, thorns and insects under his footsteps. In fact, the worry about being seen and caught had suppressed his worry about thorns and poisonous reptiles in the grass. Similarly, Jaya could virtually see nothing except a murky and top-heavy figure which was leading her; she was cautiously attempting to tag on his footsteps. The crunching and rustling noise produced by the grass under their feet was scratching its claws on the innocent silence of the night. But, Sathe Nagar, being unaware of this happening, was engrossed in profound slumber. Soon they successfully crossed the pasture, but now they had to make their way through the densely peopulated area.

The area was a labyrinth of houses; houses after houses, houses facing houses in a crowded way and through them, there laid a puzzling web of narrow alleyways. Therefore, they found it too risky to carry the cadaver openly from there and so they stopped. Having a heavy load on the back, gasping Vikas had stood trying to figure out some working way but his agonized body and the fear of approaching dawn were hasting and hassling him to make his mind quicker and hence he could produce nothing out of his thinking.

Eventually, Jaya suggested him to move on by the back side of the houses and thus they stealthily walked by the shadows of the walls. While passing by some of houses, they heard someone gargling, someone coughing, someone pouring water, and some mother consoling her crying infant. This made them aware that every house was not asleep; some of houses had started their daily routine too. This notice doubled up their nervousness.

After fifteen minutes' backbreaking walk, they reached the middle of the area and found themselves in a quandary, because their way ahead was right through the interfacing lines of houses. And now, they had neither time to think of some other way nor a substitute to move back. Jaya suggested him that they should leave the body where they were standing and they should flee. But, as he did not want to leave back any clue, he declined the suggestion.

Subsequently, Vikas took it as a do-or-die situation and marched forward right through the lanes of houses.

On either sides of the way people had slept in their foreyards, and right through them the couple was carrying the corpse. Both of them were frightened and nervous. He knew that even a slightest careless movement or noise could alarm the people about their presence. Therefore he was walking with great efforts and caution.

Due to the burden on his back his fragile body was almost bowed and by-and-by it was getting exhausted; his shivering hands were losing their holds; his falteringly stepping legs were not at all able to bear the burden anymore; his heart was desperately demanding for long breaths. Nevertheless, he was sneakily passing by the sleeping heads without gasping and grunting. She could perceive her husband's condition but she was helpless. She was worried lest he should lose his balance and collapse on any of the men sleeping beside the way.

Suddenly, a dog, slept beside men, picked up their presence. It stared at the couple for a while as if it was confirming whether they were any strangers and then gave a shrill bark, which alerted the other sleeping dogs. And, in no time a pack of dogs, while shattering the silence of the night with their rigorous collective barking, wildly paced towards them in a mood of attack. Seeing the advancing dogs, both of them remained terrified and bewildered; she noisily asked him, 'Run..run..run! Drop him down and run!' But, before he could do so, the dogs surrounded them and from every side every dog doggedly tried to get the honour of being the first to lick the blood of the prey.

The spouses were frenetically moving around while sweeping their hands and legs to keep the dogs away, but those stray dogs were too stubborn and cunning. They were frightening the couple by bearing their jack-knife like teeth and by growling at them furiously. However, while the couple dealt with an attacking dog, the other two would take its advantage and would cunningly try to attack them from the other sides. In this game, one of dogs caught Vikas's calf, pierced its long teeth in his flesh deeply and then with a jerk pulled out little flesh of his calf, but he dumbly bore its pains.

The dogs, with their barking, growling and wailing, ruffled the peace of the night thoroughly and caused a hindrance in the sugary sleep of the people. Getting irritated to the noise, a man got up to run away the dogs but after seeing the scene he himself started shouting 'Thieves...Thieves ....thieves! Wake up! Catch them.. Catch them!'

In a fraction of minute, the entire area woke up and rushed towards the couple shouting 'Hey you, don't run! Catch them..Kill them... Hack their feet!'

Seeing a multitude of people running towards them with sticks, axes and swords in their hands, Vikas and Jaya nearly died with the frustration of upcoming calamities. Soon, the dogs ran away and the people took their positions but before somebody could assault the couple, Badal shouted, 'Hey! Don't beat them, they are not thieves, he is our Vikas and his wife.' Chndya asked Vikas, 'Vikas, but at this odd time what are you doing here and what is there in the sack?' Vikas was frightened and tired, he placed the sack down and then replied calmly, 'I have just come from the long trip and there is nothing in the sack except toys. And, as the sack was too heavy, i kept the material beside the road and fetched her to help me in carrying it. That's it'

Thus in a perfectly organized way he gave a convincing reply. The excited crowd was then subdued and shortly it dispersed. Vikas and Jaya both of them were tremendously relieved. Her eyes brimmed with tears. He noticed them and consoled her by blinking his eyes to her. Subsequently, Badal, Altaf and Motiram Appa offered him help so as to take the sack to his home, but he kindly declined their help.

Now as almost all the people were awakened. In many of the foreyards people had sat chatting, so the spouses had no other option than carrying the corpse back to their home. So, he picked up the sack on his back and walked towards his home while she followed him dumbly with many questions and worries burning in her mind. When they approached the house, he asked her, 'Keep the can of kerosene in the house and fetch the crowbar and a container. I think this scoundrel wants to decay in the ground. We will bury him in Malte's field. Come there quickly.' She nodded her head positively and left.

Swiftly she reached the field with the articles. Then, as the day was about to break, they hurriedly dug a pit and before the day broke, they buried Raja in it and returned back to their home quietly.

Raja's sudden disappearance had shocked everyone and caused hustle-bustle in the area. It had been a serious topic of discussion among the people. His house was under the shadow of sorrow and surprise. His mother and wife, with tearful eyes and bruised hearts, were agitatedly waiting for him. However, when the house would merge in the darkness of the midnight, a strange mournful humming of his mother would echo in the dumb and deserted locality.

His all kith and kin were tirelessly searching for him; Rakmaji Bhau had been constantly pressurizing police for finding out his crony but all the resources had proved to be futile.

It was afternoon, as people had gone to work and children to school, the entire locality was as dead as a desert. In such a gloomy ambience, Vikas, lying on the cot, was profoundly engrossed in his thoughts and Ragh, propping her back against the wall, had sat near the door dumbly. There was a strange melancholic mood in the house.

'I don't know why, but these days i feel very much insecure in this house; i feel suffocating here!' her hesitatingly delivered dialogue scattered the silence and opened a talk. On this, he clearly declared, 'Raja is over, now it's that Haramkhor, Rakmaji's turn! Until i tear his heart, i won't move anywhere!' She softly said, 'But what i say.' 'You better say nothing!' he angrily interrupted her and closed the talk. And again silence took over the house.

After sometimes, Ravi poured in while shouting, 'Dada..!..Dada! That Raja Mama, who used to come to our house, has died!' Listening to this news, the husband and the wife remained openemouthed. Further, before they could ask him something, the boy voluntarily added, 'And you know Daa! The murderer had very badly shattered Raja's chest and had buried him in Malte's field but stray dogs unearthed his body; they too tore it very badly! Now a posse of policemen has arrived there!' On this, they stared at each other's face shockingly and then noisily rushed out of the house to see the happening.

Standing in the foreyard of the house, Vikas and Jaya could view the distal picture of the spot.

School children who were just on their way to home for the lunch-break were curiously pouring towards the field with their bizarre noise. The ones who had a glance over the corpse were flooding back with a horror in their eyes and a sort of disgust on the faces. The mournful howling and bawling of the dead one's family was echoing in the vicinity and collecting more and more people there. Soon, Rakmaji and his comrades too barged in the scene and remained stupefied after seeing the scoured and tottered body of their friend who had laughed and gossiped with them just two or three days back.

Rakmaji's sentiments for Raja were spontaneously overflowing; he was moaning with dry-eyes saying, 'I lost my right hand; he was purer than gold! Even the affection of a thousand of friends after my own heart would be as trivial as an eye of the ant before the Himalayan-pile of his love for me!' Then, he turned to the police inspector and said to him, 'Sahib, until the murderer has been hanged to death, i and my comrades are going to be your regular shadow. To this, the police inspector nodded with an assuring look, asked his subordinates to scan the spot thoroughly and collect all the micro and macro evidences found in the search. The dead body was sent to the city hospital for the post-mortem.

LAYER – 43

A week later, Raja's wife delivered a baby and with the arrival of this little seraph, the dark cloud of sorrow, which had overcast the house, received a brilliant silver lining in the form of this newly born baby. In a way, it proved to be a solacement to the family.

However, in case of Raja, life had taken a dramatic turn; he always wished to have a boy-child, but every time his destiny dismayed him by giving him girl-child after girl child. But now, after four girls his wish was fulfilled but unfortunately he was no more to see his son.

Now Jaya and her family had shifted to her maternal town, Parandha and by the courtesy of her mother, they were trying to rehabilitate there.

Here, yet the police inspector had got no trace of the culprit, and every now and then Rakmaji Bhau was questioning and croaking him for the deferment in the search. Besides, he , through Jophle Sahib, was mountaining pressure on the cop. Therefore, having exasperated beyond his endurance, the cop disparately wanted to wrap up this case anyhow and get rid of this regular headache. For that he had the only strategy to use; in fact this particular strategy has always been a reserved and useful weapon for the corrupt cops when they undergo pressure and fail to find a real culprit.

He asked his assistants to find out the person in the area who had any sort of verbal or physical tussle with the dead one.

Thus, at the battle-level-emergency, as per the instruction the team of assistants investigated people in the area and fetched a scapegoat to the police station as a suspect on the ground of nothing but simply for he was abused by the dead one in the trance of wine for no reason. And, the parody was that the victim was not even told on what charge he was arrested.

 'What's your name?' the police inspector asked the suspect piercingly. The suspect grabbed the inspector's feet and pleaded 'Sahib, on the oath of your sacred feet i tell you, i have done nothing! Please, let me go, I am a poo...' 'Hey Bhadkhav! You bluff-crafty! Stop your foxiness at once and just answer my question!' barked the inspector at him and quieten him. The subdued suspect answered in lower voice, 'Sahib, Badal!' The inspector friendly kept his hand on Badal's shoulder and said to him softly, 'Badal Bhau, i know you haven't done anything wrong. In fact it's natural; in the trance of wine a man can't control his emotions and actions, can he?' Although Badal couldn't understand what the cop was talking about, he nodded his head bewilderedly and frighteningly so as to respond to the cop. Then the inspector asked his subordinate to bring a cup of tea for Badal. He requested Badal to sit on the chair and have the tea. This hospitality made Badal feel grateful but immensely uncomfortable to sit on the chair in front of the inspector, but he obeyed the instruction. However, while having tea he was feeling so awkward that even the special and sweet tea tasted like boiled water and nothing. Somehow he voided the cup, kept it down and looked at the cop disarmingly. The cop too responded similarly and spoke, 'In fact, you should not regret for what you have done. Had Raja or someone else ever abused me, one hundred and hundred percent i tell you that i would have chopped him up to minced mutton.' Badal smiled politely and again nodded to show his agreement to what the cop said and then asked, 'Sahib, now may i go!' 'Aare, how can you go like this? Now, you are our son-in-law, means our special and permanent guest!' spoke the inspector naughtily. At this time, wrinkles of worries emerged on Badal's brow; he desperately requested the cop, 'Sahib, i am a poor being, please, don't rag me or i will die!' On this, the cop burst into a fake laughter and then while controlling himself, he asked the victim, 'You just tell me whether you have your own shelter to stay.' Badal mutely shook his head in despair. Subsequently, the cop asked, 'Okay, and, what about your food? I mean, from where do you get it?' Badal, who had been sitting lowering his head at the thought of what he had to face, looked up at the cop dumbly; his deeply sunken eyes reflected the unspoken agonies of his life and the horror of future. While waiting for Badal's oral answer, the cop glanced over the victim's flimsy body, which very much seemed like a scarecrow wrapped in some torn and overused slack cloths. But, Badal remained speechless. Then, the cop sympathetically kept his hand on Badal's dropped shoulder and said to him, 'See Badal, you have neither a shelter to dwell nor any assurance of food, but here you have a shelter, two times full meal, breakfast and tea. What else you want to live!' To this, Badal joined his hands and spoke humbly 'No..no..not at all Sahib! Even if someone gives me Panchpakwan (Royal food) to eat every day and a luxurious bed to sleep, i won't be alive within four walls! Sahib, more than three quarters of my life i have spent half hungrily in the open like a withered, leafless and isolated tree, and now i am acclimatized to this way of living life. Besides, the death is just at a hand-distance and now i have nothing to do except waiting for her to embrace me in her arms! I am happy. There are many needy people like me, let some of them get the benefit of this scheme.' Now, the police inspector wrathfully stood and shouted at Badal, 'Aare Yedpatta (mad)! It is a police station not a Vrudhashram (orphanage for old people) to help needy people. You better understand, we have arrested you on the charge of Raja's murder. Now, stop your coquettishness and straightaway confess the offence and sign the statement. Already, i have entertained you a lot. But now i have neither time nor patience for that.' This strange emphatic accusation shocked Badal so sharply that for a while he could see nothing except revolving, blurred and fragmented images of the things around him. As soon as he recovered from it, he kept his old white head on the inspector's shoed feet and broke down imploring, 'No, it's not true! Aieshapath (On the oat of my mother) I haven't killed anyone! Sahib, i agree, sometimes i steal hens but i have killed no human! You have misunderstood me! Sahib, have mercy upon this tired old man! Believe me, I haven't done it!' The inspector spoke, 'See Badal, every culprit does the same thing that you are doing now for winning our sympathy and trust, but let me tell you, you are in vainly burning your fuel because we have dearth of mercy and sympathy. We have many other better ways and means of detecting the truth and making the culprit confess it. But, i don't want to annoy you so you too don't; just, accept the crime without any fuss and co-operate us. I assure you, here you will find your life better than outside.' But, Badal refuted this proposal and assertively told the cop that he had not committed this crime so at any cost he would not accept it.

Eventually, the cop secretly beckoned to his men and they

immediately grabbed Badal and dragged him inside towards the special cell. While this weak old victim, like a newly school going child, miserably howled, balked and jerked in protest to this forceful act.

In the cell the police men took out his all cloths and hooked him by his abdomen onto the hanging tyre in such a manner that his buttocks would face the ceiling. All the time the poor man was piteously weeping and earnestly appealing for letting him off. Subsequently, a police man warned him to accept the crime and the moment he got Badal's negative reply, he banged a huge fiber-stick on the victim's bony rump so violently and vigorously that the old man outshouted and urinated in sync. Seeing it another policeman got stimulated and joined the first one exclaiming, 'Waa...what a shot..! Jhatkyat mutawlach! Now, until he says yes, we won't stop; peel out the skin of his bottom, hum.. Start! Kar chalu... (start)!' Thus, those two policemen, one after another, were thrashing his hindquarters with the sticks in the passion a washer-man bangs cloths on a washing-stone. Every wallop was so tormenting that Badal was hoarsely and wildly screaming and wailing out of agonies, however the brutal men, being envious of each other, were mechanically and recurrently grunting 'Hum..! Hum!' for discharging more vigorous thwack than the previous one and barking at the victim angrily 'say yes!' Eventually both the policemen became dead beats, so the other two took over the victim; one of them fetched a packet of red chili powder, mixed it in a mug of water and splashed that pungent red concoction on the pilled and swollen skin of old Badal's base, and the victim, having felt as if somebody had set his base on flames, utterly screamed to give vent to the intense burning and throbbing sensations. Notwithstanding, the policeman once again asked him to accept the crime and for getting no reply, he wrathfully took a handful chili powder and rubbed it wildly on the same smashed and puffed-up skin and despite Badal's groaning and shrill screaming, he again whipped the same part cruelly with the stick until he himself got tired. Horrified Badal was simply shivering with pains; his throat and lips were dried. He had no more strength to shriek or cry; his head was whirling; in his sight everything was blurred and was revolving around him. His fragile and aged physique could no longer bear the agonizing treatment and soon he became unconscious. So the policeman rested his stick while the other took his turn; he splashed a mug of water on old Badal's face and shouted, 'Ye Haramkhor! Ooth!' so raucously that the victim shuddered and at once opened his eyes wide and started weeping piteously. The stone-hearted policeman could not at all be susceptible to the old victim's pitiful condition, on the contrary he furiously kicked and whipped the victim with his belt while the victim lying helplessly could only produce painful commotions.

Eventually, being thwarted in attaining the goal, the irritated policemen further lay him on a slab of ice by his stomach and began to express their frustration in the form of a violent thrashing to Badal. Skin-crushing and bone-vibrating hits of the sticks along with the coating of red chili powder on every wound left by the sticks and the flesh piercing chillness of the ice on the front entirely tormented Badal. Now he was unable to put up with this excruciating torture. At last, in order to get rid of the hellish pains, he glaringly mumbled, 'Ye..s, i kil..led Raja, but sto..p now' and then the banging of sticks died down. The panting policemen being perspired threw the sticks in a corner and swiftly walked out for cooling themselves. While the poor being lay alone in the cell weeping bitterly and feeling weak and all alone in this oppressive world.

Thus for saving his own cap, the disgusting cop used his rights unethically and unlawfully and attributed the crime on an innocent person forcefully. Moreover, on the very day he announced his accomplishment in a diplomatic and dignified manner.

Badal's condition was so deteriorated that he could neither sit by his base nor slip by his back therefore most of the time he would lie by his stomach on the bare floor and would wail painfully day and night. However, more than his physical pain he was distressed for being deprived of wine; the agitation of his flesh and soul would sometimes escalate so desperately that in the fit of hysteria he would lay on the floor paralyzed shivering and draining saliva from his ill-turned and twisted mouth for hours and hours. But in such conditions also no policeman would bother to see what had happened to the old man.

After a fortnight Badal was taken to the city court for hearing. Badal who could walk with great difficulty was in huge iron shackles, hand-cuffs and fetters, which weighed heavily on his frail and bony body. Moreover, two sturdy policemen had held him by the shackles as if he were an untamed burly bull. As his hearing was in the queue, the cop instructed his men to wait in the foreyard of the court and went away.

While the policemen along with Badal were waiting for their call, by chance Chandya saw Badal and swiftly approached him. The unspoken pains and horror on Badal's wrinkled and tired face; buzzing and flittering flies around the countless scars and wounds on his body; unkemptly long- grown hair on his head and a cluster of rumpled beard below his dried and cracked lips and   a reflection of being alone and helpless in his deep-gone ruddy eyes moved Chandya's heart and moisturized his eyes. Similarly, on seeing someone from his place, Badal's feeling of self-pity and homesickness surfaced spontaneously and he could not refrain himself from bursting into tears. While breathing half he moaned, 'Chandya, my brother, in the name of Lakshimi Aie , bring me a bottle of poison, i will have it, and will get rid of that hell and the pestering of these brutal policemen! These dingoes are wildly chewing my flesh and bones bit by bit from toes to chest keeping my throat safe to breathe for being alive and to shriek painfully; I can't bear it now! I want to die...i wan...!' his last word thawed out in his impulsive outburst. Chandya stroke his back gently and consoled him saying, 'Be calm! You need not to cry, i know you are not a murderer! I will ask Rakmaji Bhau to do something for you; believe me soon you will be at Sathe Nagar.' Badal's emotions and sorrow flew through his words, 'Now it seems impossible; until i die, i can go nowhere! Anyways, brother, tell me, how is my Khandoba's temple, my Masanvata [grave yard] the cool shadow of my Neem tree on the embankment of the calm lake, the isolated and tranquil temple of Panchmukhi Maruti, the evening mirth and joy of the fellow brothers at the Wine Adda and the amusing hustle bustle of my Sathe Nagar? My life has been hellish without them. Since my boyhood I had been with them but these demons have separated us just at the time of resting this worn out body there forever. Alas! Now i will have to leave my last breath at the most disgusting place and among the heartless strangers!' 'Calm down, don't speak like a crazy brat! Rakmaji Bhau would certainly free you. And once again you will ...'

'Ye you enough, leave now!' a coarse voice of the policeman interrupted Chandya. He nodded yes to the policeman, whispered something to Badal and left.

Immediately after his departure, Badal, raising his little finger, beckoned to the policemen for using pissoir. Having expressions of irritation on their faces, the policemen took him to a lavatory; they stood at the door and asked him to go in. In the lavatory, Chandya had already been waiting for him, he briskly produced something from inside his shirt and secretly rendered it to Badal and bolted out. Badal hurriedly went in a corner, unwrapped the paper around it and smiled joyfully; it was a jumbo bottle of strong Deshi Daru [indigenous wine]. Until he unscrewed the cap with his shivering hands, the eruption of his thrust ran through him like lightning, blowing his patience up into uncountable shreds. However, no sooner did he open it than he gulped down the wine in two breaths. Now the happiness of whole world reflected on his face. In a moment his sorrow and worries vanished. Subsequently, being aware of the policemen who were waiting for him outside, he quickly threw the empty bottle in the corner and swiftly walked out normally.

Just after a few minutes, the cop called them inside. The policeman handed the charge-sheet over the judge. The magistrate glanced over old Badal who was standing before him with his submissively lowered down head and after that he looked into the paper. While going through the paper, the magistrate spoke, 'So, he has murdered.' Then, looked up at Badal and asked, 'Old man, why did you do this crime at this age?' But, Badal could not dare to utter even a letter. He stood dumb and stock-still like a statue. For a while the magistrate waited for his reply and then asked the police inspector, 'Inspector, i guess he is not dumb, is he?' On this, quietly standing Badal suddenly roared, 'Ye your baap(father) would be dumb, not i am!' These words shocked everyone and caused a lot of commotion among the people there. The inspector showed his enlarged eyes to threaten him and gestured to mind his language. But, Badal shouted at him too saying, 'Ye Kaloondrya (Black rat)! Don't show me your ratty-eyes; without knife i will take them out of your skull and will hang them to the arch of a grave-yard!' 'Old man, do you know where are you and to whom are you talking?' the magistrate furiously asked him. In reaction Badal broke out shouting at the judge, 'Ye Rranredya (wild-buffalo), Nit bol, hold your tongue! Call me Badalraao and not old man! Naad naay karaaycha Badalcha! No challenge to Badal! On the spot, on the spot i will buy you out along with the seat on which you are sitting now, and will sell off you at an auction in a Donkey-Bazaar! Ye..! Fifty six like you i have kept at my feet! Haan, Naad naay karaayach aapla!' 'Inspector, took him out at once!' shouted the magistrate irritably. The inspector and his subordinates hastily dragged him out while all the time he kept on threatening and abusing to the magistrate and to the police men who were pulling him out.

After reaching at the police station, the policemen fished out their frustration by giving Badal an intensive thrashing for his act in the court and also for making them feel embarrassed there.

They also got hold of Chandya and knocked him out severely for providing alcohol to Badal.

However, the news papers gave air to the scene in the court criticizing the police for its negligence in the work.

LAYER – 45

Since Raja's death Rakmaji had been feeling unwell. Dramatically his health had got deteriorated and day by day it was getting worst and worst. He looked weak; his overweight and plump figure had shockingly turned into a skeletal one. This abrupt change in his physique had shocked everyone in Sathe Nagar and had begotten many cat and bull stories. One of them was that he was haunted by Raja. However, unfortunately it was not a rumour but it was the prophecy of a devotee-foreteller of Lakshimi Aie, Mala Maie. She had told Rakmaji Bhau that after a long sleep Raja's soul had awakened and it was dreadfully thirsty of blood, and for satisfying its thirst, its evil eyes had befallen on him. However, she had tried all the means and strategies for dissuading the evil-spirit from Rakmaji but she could bring no improvement to Rakmaji's physical condition. So she had openly warned Rakmaji saying, 'Terrible, even five goats' blood couldn't satisfy him! He is terribly powerful! He wants to suck your blood to death. And perhaps, no devotee, no saint and no doctor can deter him from doing so!' And, these very words had implanted horror and restlessness in Rakmaji's life.

Now, all the time he was living under the apprehension of death; every time he could perceive something strange around him; he was feeling insecure and restless. That's why this man, who used to hardly stay at home in day times and sometime at night too, was now all the times lying in front of an idol of Lakshimi Aie in his room like an eggs-incubating hen. And, even on hearing a slight odd sound, the man of boldness and vigour was wincing like a timid child.

Day by day, along with his health his hope of getting well was also dwindling down. But, his wife had determined to emancipate him from the thirsty hirudinean spirit at any cost. For that she would take him to Baba, Molana, Sadhu, Saint, temple, mosque, church and to everyplace where she would be given an assurance of her husband's emancipation.

After a month Badal was taken to the court, however this time, while waiting for the call in the court premises, the cop neither allowed any of Badal's acquaintances to meet Badal nor he permitted him to use a lavatory there.

Soon Badal was called in and once again he was standing before the magistrate timidly bowing his head down. Perceiving quietness in the hall, he stealthily raised his head and had a fleeting look to know why it was so. To his surprise, all the while the magistrate was wrathfully staring at none other than him while the other members were gazing at the magistrate with amazement. Badal felt tremendously awkward and so quickly he lowered his head down. The magistrate satirically busted, 'Oh Mr. Badalraao! You are welcome here, Sir. By the way, when are you going to sell me and my chair in an auction in a donkey bazaar? That day you were going to buy me out to keep at your feet, what about that?' Badal joined his hands and humbly responded to the magistrate saying 'Sahib, a destitute like me who can't buy even a pinch of poison for himself, how can he venture to speak so?' 'Do you mean you didn't say so?' asked the judge. 'No Sahib, not at all!' politely but assertively Badal denied. 'Then who said, your ghost!' shouted the judge. Badal trembled convulsively and stood tight-lipped. The other people in the court too were awfully subdued and silent. The justice had been waiting for his reply while all the time Badal had been staring at the ground at his feet silently. Everyone's eyes had concentrated on Badal. After a while the justice, having no response from the culprit, ordered him, 'Now, don't be dumb, speak up.' This time Badal looked at the magistrate and implored, 'Sahib, it was not me, actually it was the wine in me which spoke with you rudely! This is the truth, Sahib!'

On this childish reply people burst into laughter. The magistrate sighed and asked irritably 'Great heavens! Aren't you ashamed of this hypocritical demeanour?' 'No Sahib, I mean i am not telling any lies!' 'But, it was not the wine, it was you who had drunk it willingly, hadn't you?' 'No Sahib, i swear by my died aunt; i didn't go to her, she came to me!' To this people ridiculously laughed at him. The magistrate asked the cop, 'Inspector, even today has he drunk?' 'No sir, today i did not allow him to go even to a lavatory,' reported the inspector. Again the justice turned to Badal and asked, 'Okay Badal, so you say wine itself came to you, don't you?' 'Yes Sahib!' 'Can you tell me how it came to you? I mean whether it came to you on its own feet or by bus or by plane or it rode to you on a horse.' 'Sahib, it rode to me. It rode to me on my friend, i mean in his pocket.' 'So you saw it and asked your friend for it, didn't you?' 'Yes, i asked but for water and not for wine.' 'Badal, are you overdoing?' 'No Sahib' 'Then while drinking, couldn't you differentiate between water and wine?' 'Sahib, the bore -well water for the prisoners in the jail and hatbhatti [local wine] both of them taste alike so i could find nothing wrong with it. Similarly, due to taking bath with cold water every day in the bitter winter i had got so severe cold that my nose was almost blocked with mucus. Sahib, those days i was not breathing by my nose but i was doing it by my mouth. That's why I couldn't even smell it. Sahib, but it doesn't mean that i couldn't make it out.' Further he continued in a lower but serious tone, 'The reality is i understood what i was drinking and even i knew the fact that if i drank it, i wouldn't be able to tell you that i haven't murdered anyone and i would be hanged to death for no fault of mine. The thought of getting sentenced to death entirely hollowed my heart; i begged and warned myself not to drink her that day. However, the treacherous temptation of consuming her coaxed me to have her. Initially it wooed just for two sips of wine and after that every time it kept me luring to have just two more until the bottle was over. This temptation deceived me! Sahib, my addiction sold out my conscience!' The justice suspired and said, 'And, the same addiction made you kill Raja, didn't it, Badal?' 'No Sahib, believe me, i am a drunkard but not a murderer!' 'But Badal, i have your recorded statement in which you have already accepted the offence and on that basis you are a culprit.' 'No Sahib, that's not the truth!' 'If it was not truth, why did you accept it then?' 'Sahib, this inspector Sahib asked me whether I murdered Raja or not and i told him the truth, 'no', but Sahib, he and his men thrashed me to faint for saying so. On the one hand they kept on grilling me for the truth and on the other hand on obtaining my 'no' the truth, they went on whipping me with their battens so harshly that my skin was peeled off and the flesh under it was smashed. Yet, they kept on flogging it and for making it worst, they rubbed red chili powder on my smashed flesh widely! Then, I understood that the truth that the cop expected from me was to make me tell the untruth, 'yes'. I knew only the word 'yes' could assuage me from their torture, nonetheless, i kept on telling him the truth, 'no'. But after a while, when blood in the wounds absorbed the chili powder and the huge battens and belts rigorously kept on knocking out my nude crushed skin, my earthly body, having overwhelmingly harassed by those excruciating pains, desperately agitated for a relief. I pathetically begged them for mercy; i cried bitterly and screamed agonizingly. Sahib, i tossed and trembled with pains but these Gods of butchers kept on drilling my welts and wounds. And eventually, wooing to the anguish, my mouth voluntarily sounded off 'yes', the untruth and the battens and belts stopped as they got what they wanted from this weak and old man!' 'See Badal, the fact is every culprit claims to be innocent; however police don't have any magical wand to detect the truth, hence they have to be a bit of strict and violent while investigating criminals. Nevertheless, I order the police inspector to reinvestigate the case. But meanwhile Badal will remain in the police-custody. All right the next case,' the justice said professionally while looking into some papers.

The two heavy policemen efficiently marched forward, held Badal by his arms and walked towards the door. While walking Badal murmured to himself, 'This system is weaker and more illiterate than me yet it is correct. Why? Because, literate people run it. Police don't have magical wand to detect the truth so they have government licenses to beat and behave harshly with anyone!'

LAYER – 47

Those days Rakmaji was behaving strangely. He would startle awake in the midnight and would savagely scratch and bite his own hands and would suck his own blood. Sometimes, in darkness of the night he would wander in Sathe Nagar. While loitering he would open anyone's birdhouse or a goat-shed and grabbing hens and lambs, he would wildly cut their throats with his teeth and would voraciously suck their blood. After having drunk to his satisfaction, he would escape from there with the mouth smeared with blood. Besides, he would go to Smashan Bhoomi (crematorium) and standing before a burning dead body, he would painfully wail and whimper. And, when there would be no burning cadaver, he would either sleep in the heap of ashes in the crematory or he would apply the ashes on his entire body and would nakedly ramble in the dark and isolated forest while whimpering and laughing notoriously all the time.

These inhuman and abnormal activities of Rakmaji had harassed his wife and sons and had created a sort of terror in people's minds. His sons, for keeping watch on him, could neither sleep properly nor eat at ease; every now and then they would run after him for fetching him back to home. However, just a blink or a nod of their watchful eyes would be enough for Rakmaji to deceive them and to escape from their detention.

Resultantly, almost every morning some or the other person would come to them shouting, abusing and grumbling about Rakmaji's evil deed with a carcass of his or her animal in the hand which would be killed the previous night. Therefore, his wife, being annoyed by the people's grievances and curses, had then started to lock him in a room.

But, after being imprisoned in a room, the wildness of his anger had touched the sky. Now, whoever would go into the room for feeding him, he would bare his teeth and growl at the person like a beast and would violently assault the person. Similarly, during a day time he would cry pathetically like a child lost in a fair, but in the midnight he would roar and howl like a blood-thirsty wild beast; although he had no much strength in his body, yet he would hurl himself on the wall and hit his head on the walls in an attempt to break the confine.

Once he banged his head so hard that it started bleeding, yet in the frustration he kept it banging in quick succession. By the time his sons ran to stop him, his forehead was daubed with blood; from every side of his head drops of blood were rolling down on his cheeks, nape and nose. His both sons together with their all strength were trying to hold him back but surprisingly enough the thin and weak man, like a sturdy and uncontrolled horse, was pushing and tossing them away while screaming wildly and agonizingly all the time. His beastly wailing and whimpering were so piercing that they echoed in the vicinity and shook the silence of the midnight. Even the flocks of crows and cranes which were resting on the trees noisily and frighteningly fluttered their wings and flew away with mayday crowing and cooing. Even the people in the area ghastly woke up and surged to Rakmaji's home to see what was going on.

LAYER – 48

Three months had elapsed since Jaya had left her home. Her children and husband had well settled at the new home, but unfortunately the maternal climate did not suit her. Immediately a month after shifting, her husband went on his toy-selling trip and since then she had been bedridden. In the beginning, once her mother had taken her to the civil hospital, there the doctor gave some medicines and asked her to undergo some physical tests which were very expensive for them. That time Jaya told her mother that the illness was casual and temporary, and in a few days it would itself be cured without any medical treatment. She further told that she had lived her life, but her children had yet a lot to see and do. Therefore, she would prefer her death to spending money on the medicines and undergoing such expensive tests by starving her children. And thus, surrendering herself to her fate, she came back home.

In a short course of time, she became so weak that she couldn't even stand on her own; her limbs appeared as bony as bamboo branch-sticks besides her fleshless forehead and cheekbones were studded with pus-vomiting ringworm-welts which looked ridiculously ugly on her face. Day and night she would cough glaringly.

However, in this critical time her mother was with her that's why Jaya was worriless about her motherly duties. But, after undergoing a prickling and hard time, when it was time to live peacefully and happily with her family, the sudden illness had befallen on her as the worst curse and deprived her of this happiness. This particular fact was pinching her inwardly.

That day Vikas was to come back home, hence since morning Jaya's sight and soul had been hanging around the road. Now, it was night, her mother asked her to have supper, but Jaya refused to do so saying that she [Jaya] and Vikas would dine together. Her mother told her that his homecoming was uncertain that day so she should not kick his heels. 'Just more half an hour, Aie! If he doesn't come by then, i will have' with these soft words she persuaded her mother. Then, her mother served food to the children, the children had it and went to their bed. The mother washed the used utensils and tidied up the room, yet there was no trace of his arrival. Finally her mother forcefully fed Jaya and took her to the bed in the house and she too kept herself down beside the children in the foreyard.

On the lap of aged night, the garrulous houses were now calmly asleep by embracing silence in their arms, but Jaya, lying alone in the house, was staring outside in the darkness through the open door. The speechless sound of the midnight was poking into her heart with her own restlessness and depression.

While, at a little distance in the darkness an imprecise image of some person floated on her eyes. She surprisingly peered into the darkness to know who it was, but she couldn't make it out. However, she perceived that someone having wrapped itself from head to knee in a blanket was rapidly advancing towards the house.

This discovery begot a doubt in her mind as whether he was her husband or someone unwanted and unexpected...

No sooner did she blink her eyes than the person was standing at the door. 'Jaya, i have come!' She heard this familiar sound and her nerviness replaced with cheerfulness. She laughed at herself and murmured, 'Haa! It is he! How badly i desired to see my husband! Lakshimi Aie, you listened to the voice of my heart! May your name perpetuate so long as the sun and moon are alive!'And then, she noisily lifted her upper body, painfully reclined it on her elbows, smilingly glanced over him and at once the smiling look switched to the furrowed brow and lowered eyes as his face was strangely muffled to his eyes. She couldn't understand why he had done so. But, in spite of having this 'why' in her mind she hospitably asked him to come in and placed her pillow at a hand distance for him to sit. He walked in mechanically and sat on the pillow dumbly by facing the same direction as she had been. After that, she asked carefully, 'Why have you muffled to eyes? Are you not feeling well?' 'Humm' he roared like a demon. On listening to this strange vocal she startled. His odd and dry behaviour fed her doubt as whether he was her husband or someone else in the disguise of him. She then hesitatingly asked him, 'I thi..nk you have got so..ur-throat, haven't.. you?' In reply he nodded gently to indicate his agreement while gazing at the door mysteriously all the time. Later, she asked him, 'Now, draw off your blanket and bring out your face. I wish to see you to my satisfaction.' But to her amazement, this time he neither roared nor gestured in response to her demand, on the contrary he sat fixing his gaze outside in the darkness as if he was waiting for someone to come. The silence and his outlandish appearance were frightening her. In the meanwhile, a dog let out a deep throated and painful whimpering siren and then a massive moaning filled her with creepy feelings. Suddenly, he perceived something in the darkness and he too began wailing painfully as on someone's death. On seeing this strange happening, she was utterly bewildered and terrified, nonetheless she asked him in a shivering voice, 'Wh..oo aar.. yoo..?' On this, while weeping painfully and breathing shortly he bleated, 'Your death!' 'Haa! What! Let me see who the hell you are!' yelping surprisingly and horrifyingly she stretched her hand, drew off his blanket, saw the uncovered face and remained open mouthed. She couldn't believe in what she was seeing; a woman, precisely looking like her, having scattered locks of hair on and around her face, was sobbing while looking at Jaya from the corners of her eyes. She then began mourning acrimoniously, 'Now the death, stretching its mouth widely open, is riding to you to engulf you! Jaya, you are a temporary guest, have a last glance over your children and bid farewell to your husband, to your mother and to your earthly body, which is soon going to be destroyed by the fire flames at the crematorium' and then she broke down.

While seeing this strange happening, Jaya gave vent to her fear in the form of a scream and opened her eyes and found the image of the mimic Jaya nowhere. Subsequently, while puffing heavily she turned her eyesight on her left and found her mother asking her 'Have you seen some nightmare or what?' Jaya gave an approving nod to her mother and closed her eyes once again.

Unlike usual nights that night there was no uproar of Rakmaji, that's why his elder son doubted if his father had escaped from the room by some other means. He hurriedly opened the door and saw: his father had sat in a corner shoring himself up against the wall; stretching his legs widely open; dropping his head to his right shoulder; resting his hands on either sides insensibly; the iris of his eyes had moved upwards and his mouth was spherically open. Seeing him in that condition, the boy perceived what exactly had happened to his father. He ran out hot foot and gathered his mother and some of his neighbours. The woman saw her husband and broke down uncouthly. She started beating her chest with both the hands while lamenting in a conventional singing tone, 'Gone...! My master gone! Eventually, that Naskabhadya Raja cut the thread of my husband! How the time treacherously precipitated him into the mouth of death! Someone fetch my husband back or else send me to him! Ye maza Rakmajirao gela mala sodun! Now, somebody tell me how i should live without him!' She then banged her hands on the ground and broke all the bangles in her hands. At that time, an old woman came forward and wiped off the Kunku [red powdered Bindi mostly used by married women for adorning their foreheads] on the forehead of Rakmaji's wife. This act gave air to the weeping and bewailing of the dead one's wife and the other relatives. While the sorrowful uproar of the ladies was on the peak, a man hurriedly and practically said to the men there 'Hey people now don't delay; before the corpse becomes hard and rigid, some of you quickly call all the kith and kin of it; we are going for purchasing the funeral and cremation material.' 'True.. Absolutely true! Let's go. Aare, but first ask the widow whether the corpse has to be burnt or buried,' asked another man in the crowd. 'Ok, wait, i go and ask her,' saying so the first man approached Rakmaji's wife and whispered in her ear, 'Aakka, whether you wish to burn or bury your husband.' On hearing this she shouted piteously, 'No! Don't bury my husband! You, burn him and tomorrow bring me a pinch of his ashes so that i would mix it in a pinch of poison and would go after him!' She was acrimoniously crying. Meanwhile, one of the neighbours who was a veterinarian by profession made his way to the dead one through the crowd and just for an assurance, he once checked Rakmaji's pulse and shouted, 'Ye stop crying, he is alive! Because of a hysteric attack he might have become unconscious. At once take him to a hospital.' On hearing these words the people looked at each other's face surprisingly. Rakmaji's wife hastily ran to him and started him fanning with the loose end of her sari saying 'My Lakshimi Aie listened to me! She has fetched my husband back! Once again she has put life in my husband!' The people around quickly carried him to a hospital. At hospital, doctors checked him and admitted in ICU.

LAYER – 50

After three days, Rakmaji became conscious and everywhere in Sathe Nagar a wave of this news billowed. Gradually the hospital was filled with folk-visitors.

Having hit by the news, Chandya too rushed to see Rakmaji. On seeing Rakmaji's pathetic condition, Chandya's eyes were filled with tears. He could no longer see his chum lying in a miserable condition, so from the door itself he turned back and walked away directly to Devya's Daaru Adda.

As it was afternoon, there were only few customers in the wine Adda. With a long face Chandya asked Devya to fill a glass with wine and squatted. Devya did it and beckoned to him to take it. Chandya picked up the glass and before drinking, he glanced over the other two customers, Sanjya and Kishya who had been sitting there since morning hoping to get a glass of wine from a dupe or a kind drunkard. But unfortunately, Chandya was neither of the both for them, and they knew this fact.

Chandya, while looking at them resentfully, dipped his two fingers into the wine and sprinkled a few drops on the ground. However, the fellow-parasites shamelessly smiled their greetings to him.

While Chandya was having his drink, Sanjya asked him, 'Did you meet Rakmaji?' In response to him Chandya simply shook his head positively. Then, Kishya spoke startlingly, 'Chandya, we need to subjugate this vampire lest it should suck the people in this area to death one after another!' But, Chandya did not respond him. Next Sanjya concernedly spoke, 'Raja's wife and his newly born son both of them too have become sucked mangoes like Rakmaji Bhau!' At that time, before someone could speak, Kishya took his turn and assertively added, 'I tell you, 100 percent it is none other than Raja.' 'What makes you to be so sure about it?' Chandya asked him. 'What means, even a child in Sathe Nagar will tell you that,' Kishya added. 'What?' asked Chandya. 'That they are haunted by Raja,' answered Kishya. He then whisperingly said, 'You know whomever he haunts, like a spider he sucks his or her blood so often and so much that the victim becomes hollow and thin like a bamboo stick!'

Listening to this, Chandya looked at Devya for knowing his judgment about it, but to his amazement, he noticed that Devya, with a frowned face, was engrossed in some other thoughts. So, Chandya asked him if everything was alright. In reply, Devya, looking at him, shook his head disapprovingly and plunged his head in between his vertically positioned knees. However, Chandya understood that there was something wrong with him and so he insisted on Devya to tell why he was so much of nervous.

Eventually, Devya emerged his head from the depression between his knees, sighed and solemnly said, 'I am in the most awkward predicament!' 'Why?' asked Chandya surprisingly. 'Yaar Chandya, I need to do something to stop him or he will ruin me either of the ways!' Devya spoke agitatedly. Chandya asked, 'Who is going to ruin you and why?' 'I am really fed up! I just wanted to get rid of this regular torture, but I am unable to find a way out!' said Devya cantankerously. On this Chandya asked him to calm down and soberly said, 'Look, I will help you to do way with your problem, but for that, let me know exactly what has happened with you.'

Subsequently, Devya suspired sadly and started to narrate the incident because of which he was overwhelmingly stressed:

'A few weeks back I had slept here, while all the time some painful crying was buzzing in my ears. I could perceive someone's presence in Adda, but the slumber weighed on my eyelids so heavily that though I was awakened, I couldn't open my eyes. The crying was growing deeper and deeper and with that my restlessness too. For breaking my sleep, I jerked and jostled my head but it proved to be futile. Eventually, with closed eyes only I asked, 'Who are you?' but there was no reply. I repeated the same question thrice, but I could hear nothing except wailing and crying. However, when I asked, 'What do you want?' immediately a voice mingled in sobbing broke; it said, 'Nothing, jut.. a glass.. of wine..!' I thought he might be someone fully drunken so I strictly asked him to come in the morning. On this he furiously but emphasizing every word said, 'Now I am thirsty and only two things can fulfil my thirst – either your wine or your blood! Tell me, what do you give?' This time, to my amazement it was a familiar voice and the moment my brain paired the voice with its name, my heart missed a beat. Being partially frightened yet pretending to be bold, i seriously asked him his name. And, the moment he replied 'Ra..ja..,' my eyes opened widely on their own and I hurriedly sat up; with a frightened mind, i slowly ran my eyes from one corner to another but to my surprise there was no one. Then I understood that it was a nightmare. I looked into the wall- clock;

it was 3 am. Except clicking of the clock and whistling of nocturnal insects, everywhere there was dead silence. Finding everything normal, I thought of going to bed again. When I was just about to lie down, a whispering, 'Are you not going to serve me wine?' startled me. I pinched my hand to ensure that I was not dreaming and over and over glanced over every corner of the room to see if he was really there. But, I found every corner empty and dumb. I then hesitatingly asked if there was anyone. No sooner did I finish my words than he clearly rather furiously shouted, 'Yes, I am here right in the wall behind you! Do you want to see me how I look like after my death! Here I come, die of horror now!' 'No..No..No' I shouted horrifyingly and requested him not to appear, and for God's sake he agreed to do so.

The thought of having the wild and blood-thirsty soul right behind me, which could change its mind and grab me at any moment with its both hands, and imagining his horrible eyes, which would be staring at me through the wall, I felt same as the goat, which is locked along with a hungry lion in a cage, feels. I was bathed in sweat; my lips and throat were dehydrated out of fear. Then, he mischievously laughed and asked me if I was scared of him. I told him yes. He said to me, 'If you promise me to keep a glass of wine for me at the door every night before you go to bed, I promise you I won't harm you. What say?' That time I remembered Rakmaji's condition and thought, 'Everyday a glass for being alive is not a bad deal' and without delaying anymore I promised him to do so.' Then he stopped his narration, drank some water to wet his dried lips and mouth and then continued his talk; he fearfully told, "Then, avoiding to look at the backside wall, I went in the corner where the plastic can of wine was kept, poured wine into the glass, kept the glass out at the door and no sooner did I return back to my place than I heard, 'Devya, the glass is over, bring me another.' I quietly filled another glass, kept at the door and came back to my bed and I was just about sit, the soul said, 'the glass over, but don't bring a glass, now bring a jug.' At this time, his words made me grudge. Although I was frightened, I said, 'A jug of wine! But in the deal you said that you would take only a glass of wine.' On this he said, 'So what? Is your life so cheap?' Listening to these words, at once I gave up the protest and did as he said thinking that from the next day onwards I would never sleep there again. But the next moment, as if he read my mind told me that the day on which he wouldn't get wine, he would fulfil his thirst with my blood.

Since then he regularly comes and gulps down as many jugs of wine as he wishes. Sometimes he comes along with Nava; sometimes he brings along a crowd of his drunkard ghost-friends and empties my cans and cans of wine." He wiped his wet eyes and said, "Yielding to getting sucked to death I am any way being sucked dry by the pack of hellhounds in the moonlight and once a week by the police in the sunlight. Tell me what I should do."

On listening to this strange paranormal experience, Chandya was stupefied; he was left with no words to respond Devya's question. Kishya and Sanjya too were gravely hushed. They were simply staring at Devya's and Chandya's face alternately. After a while Chandya looked up at Devya and suggested him to go to Mala Akka. To this, Devya slipped his hand into his hip-pocket and withdrew a lemon which was crisscrossed in yellow and red with haldi and kunku, and while showing it to him he said, 'She has given it, but it does no miracle; simply unnecessary burden to carry in my pocket' further he uneasily said, 'You know, neither an enchanted lemon nor a Jadumantra can conquer that hellhound!'

This reply surprised Chandya. For a while he sat in pensive trance, perhaps, for finding some other way out to the quandary. Soon, he sighed forlornly and told Devya that he could find no other way-out than feeding the bloodsucker with liquor in lieu his blood. He then stood up and without giving a word or a look of reassurance to Devya, he started out of the shed. However, Devya, resting his head on his embraced knees, quietly kept watching Chandya through the door until he looked a minor distal figure. Once Chandya was out of sight, Devya once again sagged his head down in between his knees and plunged into the nervousness. Kishya and Sanjya beckoned to each other to leave and they too quietly set out. Now Devya was alone in the shed; only with his worries.

LAYER – 51

The doctor had given up his hope for Jaya and so a week ago he had sent her back to her home for spending her remaining time with her children.

At home, day by day her health was getting deteriorated and with it the matured death was reflecting its shadow more and more obviously on her bizarre face. Her eyes looked tired and lifeless. They were deeply sunken and filled with pity and fear. Her weak body had made her ridiculously lifeless; all the time she would simply lie in the bed helplessly.

That day, after school was over, Ravi, Sonu and Monu, her children ran into home while calling her and cheerfully embraced her wherever they could. While lying in the bed, she stroked their heads affectionately with her weak hands and while smiling asked them painfully, 'What will you do if I have to go away from you?' On this the little girls held her tightly in their tiny arms and possessively said, 'We won't let you go away from us now!' 'No Aie, please don't go back again or we will die without you like a fish dies without water!' broke Ravi seriously. He further said, 'When you were in Solapur, we cried a lot. Without you the house would look empty and deserted, in the darkness of night it would look deadly depressed; we would feel very lonely and frightened and then i, Soni and Rani would hug each other and would cry bitterly for you!' On listening to him she held them against her chest and sobbed. Resting his head on her frail shoulder the boy too sobbed saying, 'When you are at home, my legs pull me towards home, but when you were not at home I did not feel to come home!' Then little Monu spoke, 'Aie, before this Diwali you get well, we will have a lot of fun like last Diwali we had; you had made very delicious ladoos! This time too you make for us.' Jaya kissed on her cheek and nodded her head yes.

However, inwardly she was feeling guilty of being unable to give her children motherly warmth and care that they required to grow.

She had a clear hint of her death and so now her heart was burning with a thought of separation, separation from her children. Moreover, she was worried about them because they were yet not grown enough to take care of themselves when their father would be away on his trip, and now her mother was too old to look after them. Her soul had attached to her children so tightly that now she never wanted to die, never wanted to go away from them at least at that tender age of their lives. She desired to live with them and to see them growing.

The last night Rakmaji had told his wife, Damaa that he wished to have fish. So in the morning, thinking to feed her husband fish in lunch, she sent her elder son to the fish market to bring some fresh fish. Since her husband had started eating food and was behaving quit normally, her hope for his recovery had once again arisen.

Hence, that day she wanted to make fish tastier than ever. She started the preparation for cooking without having even a cup of tea lest his lunch should be late. Soon her son returned with fish. She then worked with so miraculous energy that within an hour the appetizing food was ready. She had made a variety of fish-dishes such as chili- red fish curry rich in coconut oil; golden-brownish and crispy fried fish, long grains of fried rice studded with crunchy pieces of fish; soft and succulent stuffed fish and slices of fish cooked in piquant gravy made up of garlic, onions and tomatoes. The aroma raising from these dishes had pervaded all over in the whole house; it was so delectable that the passersby breathed in deeply to satisfy their tempted tongues.

Although she felt hungry, she did not have her lunch thinking she and her husband would lunch together in the hospital. She hastily packed the food in a set of dejeuner containers, neatened her appearance without looking into the mirror and turned her tail to the hospital with the heavy set of containers.

No sooner did she enter the room than Rakmaji murmured 'fish, brought?' In reply, she just gave him an assuring look and headed towards a wheel table, which lay on his right side. In a suspended manner she turned her back towards him and covering the tower of containers on the table with her huge figure, she unbuttoned the dejeuner. While, being curious to know what she had brought in lunch, he tried to turn his damaged head to his right but it caused him a deeply piercing pain in his head so he gave up the idea and simply awaited for her while watching as much as he could through the corners of his eyes.

One by one she was opening the containers. On opening the lid of each container, the aroma of the food was springing up and spreading in the air in the room and bracing his appetite so much that he had now no pertinence to wait any further. Over and over again, he was asking her to serve him food quickly.

Soon a spectacle of the table occupied with the variety of delicious food floated in his eyesight. It filled his mouth with water and mind with greed. While staring at the food, he swallowed the saliva in his mouth; his fingers moved involuntarily, and the moment she drew the table close to him, he savagely broke out guttling one after another mouthful bite. He ate until he started nodding.

She then washed his hands, gave him some water to drink and asked him if he liked the food. To her amazement, he said to her, 'The food was incomplete.' His words pierced her mind and made her restless to know why it was not up to his expectation. She asked him, 'Did I forget to add salt to it?' 'No' answered he. 'Then, any spices?' He nodded no. Being a typical Indian wife, she felt defeated and disappointed as she had made incomplete food and so it couldn't content her husband. Afterwards, instead of asking him what there was missing in the food, she herself tasted each dish and found each dish absolutely perfect. She amazed at her husband's remark and turned towards him to ask what there was missing in the food. But, after having a heavy dose of food, he had already started snoring. This perception made her sigh as her agitation to know the reason was going to extend until he woke up.

She hastily had her lunch and sat beside him all the time staring at his face expecting him to open his eyes. Gradually, the silence in the room fell upon her eyes and in the same sitting position she too drowsed.

After about two hours, she startled awake when her elder son walked into the room to relieve her from the hospital duty. She then agonizingly moved her complaining neck, glanced at her husband who had been yet asleep, with heavy steps collected the containers in a bag and quietly started her way to home. But, after passing over the door she felt something so she turned back and asked her son, 'Sanja, when your Anna will wake up, ask him why he did not like the food. Anyways, I am coming at night but you ask him' and she left whispering something.

It was 8 pm, yet Rakmaji had been asleep. The boy, having no one to talk to and nothing to do, had become sick of sitting in that quiet and lonely room. For escaping from that prison, he had been anxiously waiting for his mother.

Meanwhile, he noticed that his father had stopped snoring, so he went closer to him, observed his face minutely and a scary doubt floated on the boy's mind; it escalated his heartbeats. To get rid of this fear he moved his father by his arm to wake him up, but his father's hand dropped off lifelessly and bit by bit the fear and shock eaten the boy up completely. He stood paralyzed staring at his father with horrified eyes and opened mouth. At that time, his mother came and on seeing her, his chocked feelings poured out and he broke down. It took no time for her to understand what had happened. She gave an outcry and the entire hospital shrank into the room to see what wrong had happened. A doctor followed by a crowd of nurses thrust ahead into the room to control the situation; the doctor attended the patient while a few nurses took over the patient's wife and tried to quieten her. However, the death had already engulfed Rakmaji. The only leftover was his sinful body, which was too going to be turned into a heap of ashes soon. Hence, neither the doctor could awaken the dead one nor the nurses could refrain the widow from bewailing and screaming.

Subsequently, the dead-body was wrapped in a white cotton cloth and was sent home. As the relatives from distal places were to come, the men decided to take the funeral in the morning.

That night there was no electricity supply in the locality. Except the flickering glow of candles and lamps shining through windows and doors everything was merged in the darkness. Besides, the weather was too windy, in the sky swift flashes of lightning, with their uncouth frightening laughter, were wriggling like snakes and exposing the houses hidden under the thick blanket of darkness; water was pouring and pouring and covering the land with slush and water.

The body was sat propping against the front wall in the veranda and the widow, sitting beside it, was inconsolably lamenting and wailing. While, the neighbors and relatives had sat around them to mark their presence. Some of them were gossiping about the dead one; some were talking about the political situation in the town; few of them were nodding; a few women, having touched by the widow's mourning, were boohooing convulsively by covering their faces with the loose ends of their saris and the ones who were interested in neither of the activities had sat with the frowned faces not because of the heartache on Rakmaji's death, but because of the boredom caused by the self imposed social duty.

Despite the unyielding rain and darkness, more and more umbrellas were rushing towards Rakmaji's house while squashing mud under their feet and producing squish swash rhythm. With the arrival of every close relative, the declined uproar would rise up and again in few minutes it would decline. Throughout the night the weeping and grieving kept on climbing up and down.

Finally the dawn broke and the rain also reduced to drizzling. Then, men hastily arranged things for the funeral rite. They gave him the last bath, put on him new cloths; adorned his forehead with white, red and black furrowed lines.

Soon Rakmaji was on the funeral-carrier ready to go to his last destination. Four people shouted the ritual hymn; 'Ram naam satya hai' and sticks banged on haalkis [traditional instruments]. The vicinity echoed with its thumping tune accompanied with the howling and cries of the relatives. Although it was raining, relatives, pals and even foes of the departed soul had come to have a last walk together with the dead fellow and to bid him farewell. The four men, repeating the hymn, picked up the carrier on their shoulders and thus Rakmaji set on his journey.

At Smashan Bhoomi, people laid the body on the pyre and performed the cremation ceremony. When the elder son lighted the pyre up, cries and screaming of the agonized hearts broke.

Meanwhile, the people in the funeral scattered into several groups; most of them sat in the public hall in front of the crematorium, some of them sat under trees and the curious ones stood around the crematory.

Almost every group was talking about the dead one. In that crowd, a couple of men too were whisperingly talking on the same subject. One of them said, 'Raja has casted his evil eyes on Sathe Nagar. How horribly he is haunting people - sucking their blood to death. Rakmaji is over, now he has caught his own wife and I heard Vikas's wife is also on the verge of death.' In between, another man excitingly added, 'Aare haa! That day my brother-in-law saw her and Vikas in the Solapur Civil Hospital. He was shocked to see her condition- dead and bony like a witch-doll made up of straws!' 'And, I can tell you on bet she is the prey in the same beast's clench,' said the first man.

The veterinarian, Rakmaji's neighbour, was listening to their conversation passively, but after the last comment he went forward to them and smilingly said, 'Brothers, but I know exactly who killed Rakmaji and how.' His sudden approach baffled the men somewhat, but then the first, showing his disinterest in knowing about it, said, 'Doctor, even a child in Sathe Nagar knows that.' The veterinarian smilingly said, 'What you and the child know is not the truth.' 'Doctor Sahib, you educated people never believe even in the truth said by an illiterate person; always find faults with us,' said the second person grouchily. 'No, it's not that. I am just telling you the fact that Raja hasn't killed Rakmaji,' said the doctor softly. Then the second person categorically asked, 'If you say Raja was not feeding on his blood, why had then a sturdy man like Rakmaji become bloodless and thinner?' The veterinarian glanced at the crematory, now the pyre was set on the furious flames. He then sighed and calmly said, 'Because he was HIV+.' On listening to him they looked at each other in an awestruck wonder and beckoned to each other to confirm it, but they seemed to be doubtful about it. 'But how do you know it?' asked the first man. 'When you people were going to burn him alive mistaking him dead, I had found him alive and had taken to the hospital. Do you remember it?' asked the doctor assertively. The men shook their heads positively. He then continued saying, 'Since the day he was admitted, I had been in touch with the doctor and yet if you doubt my words, you yourselves check his reports.' Now the men were subdued but not completely convinced. Either of them was trying to magistrate the truth in his mind, but the truth of Rakmaji's death that they and the other people knew and the truth that the doctor told them were dominating each other. The doctor's words appealed to their rationality but the prophecy by Mala Akka, the devotee of Goddess Lakshimi Aie, wasn't allowing them to believe in them.

Now, golden red flames of the fire were feeding on the body and fuel and rising higher and higher while roaring and grunting. Other people had begun to move, but those three men, standing at the same place, were yet looking at the burning pyre with preoccupied minds. As the doctor knew they were perplexed, he was waiting for their queries.

In the heap of fired timbers Rakmaji was gradually reducing to ashes. Suddenly, the dead skull exploded in the fire and the men startlingly came back to the consciousness. The doctor, giving them an assuring look, was now about to leave, right then, the first man excused him and asked, 'All of sudden, how did he get HIV+?' 'It was not all of sudden; one and a half year ago he had carried it with him from Goa,' said the doctor. 'Who told you about it?' said the first one. 'In the medical inquire, he told his doctor that he had physical relation with many harlots when he had been on the Goa tour,' replied the doctor. The second person then branched another question to the last answer and asked, 'In that case, Raja's wife and Jaya's physical condition is same as Rakmaji's was; now tell what it is.' Now the doctor was bit of annoyed of their stubbornness. He said, 'Whatever it may be, but I'm sure it is not a matter of ghost, understood?' 'Then why was Rakmaji behaving like a ghost – sitting on the banyan tree in the dark forest; roaming in the midnight in the graveyard; sleeping in the ashes of deads; breaking throats of hens, lambs and even of goats by his teeth and sucking their blood like a vampire in the midnight? Was it also because of his illness?' asked the first person in an arguing tone. The doctor gently laughed at the claimant and then he calmly said, 'Brother, once again I tell you, no ghost exists and if it is ever, it's in your mind.' On this two of them shook their heads side by side to show their disapproval to what he said. The first man mockingly said, 'What you said sounds dead beat; tell us some solid reason if you have at all.' Now, the flames at the crematorium were no more young and furious, there was no one except them and being aware of it, he was reluctant to speak any further, but lest they should misinterpret his quiet departure, he decided to explain them the possible reason of Rakmaji's abnormal behaviour. He said, 'See, generally, when a person loses his hope of getting recovered, the terror of death keeps him pestering day and night; sometimes this restlessness affects his psyche to an extent of madness. And, Rakmaji too might be a victim of the same terror.' On listening to him, the men doubtfully looked at each other and then gave him a positive nod with some sort of mischievous smile.

He couldn't understand if he had persuaded them or not, but he was sure of one thing that yet the hold of superstition on them was so much tight as the clench of a boa on its prey. He too smiled at them and set on his way to home with the lost mind in his own thoughts.

For last two days, Jaya had abandoned food. Now she had given up herself to death. While lying in the bed she would simply look into a void with the eyes brimmed with tears.

At that midnight, suddenly she burst into an intense series of cough. Puff of the cough was so severe that she could not even breathe. The nonstop loud blasts of her coughing upset peace in the room and broke up everyone's sleep. For relieving her from that cough, her mother rubbed Jaya's chest while chanting names of Gods and Goddesses; Vikas ran and fetched a glass of water for her; he gently tapped on her back and tried to give her water but as she was breathlessly coughing, she couldn't drink it. In between it started bleeding through her mouth and nose, then the force of her cough subdued. Now, she opened her mouth widely and gasped for breath, it sounded as if an exhausted horse breaths heavily after a long run. Suddenly her eyes enlarged, her brow covered with sweat, her face turned paler and frightened and while gasping she began tossing and tumbling like a fish does on earth for water. On seeing their mother's suffering, children got frightened and started crying. Then, her mother too broke down. Vikas couldn't understand what to do. He tried to soothe Jaya and kept on appealing his mother-in-law and children to calm down, but none of them stopped. At that time, Jaya stretched her legs and hands and gave a last jerk; after that, she lay calmly with the opened mouth and enlarged eyes fixed at the roof. Her mother saw her and slapped her own face with both hands while lamenting, 'Flew away! My little sparrow flew away forever! Breaking up all the relations, leaving her children alone, now whom will they call mother? For God's sake, someone fetch her back, for this old mother, fetch my lost daughter back!' Vikas' heart too was set on fire, his voice was chocked to speak anything and his ears were buzzing due to the suppressed outburst; he wanted to cry, but he swallowed his all cries and sorrow and sat silently while shedding tears. Ravi, who had been sobbing, now clung to his dead mother and broke down aloud. 'Pappa, Aie is not talking to me! She is not listening to me! What happened to my Aye?' while weeping when the youngest girl implored miserably, speechless and agonized Vikas pressed her against his chest and burst into cry; he sobbed gaspingly.

LAYER – 55

After three months, once again Badal was standing in front of the magistrate for his retrial. While the magistrate was going through the reinvestigation file, Badal, being worried about the verdict, was timidly and restlessly waiting for the judge's words. When the magistrate popped his head out of the file to say something, Badal missed his heartbeat; he trembled with fear, but the magistrate's words, 'Badal, in the reinvestigation you are found innocent and so you are free now' relieved him immensely. He was increasingly happy, his eyes were brimmed with tears and gratefulness. He joined his hands, bowed before the magistrate and expressed his unspoken gratitude towards him.

He was thrilled with a thought of going back to his place and meeting his companions.

No sooner had he been set free than he belted along the way to Sathe Nagar. He was desperately eager to see his people and place. While he was walking, one after another picture of the temple of Khandoba, Panchamukhi, Neem tree on the embankment of the lake and especially images of Smashan Bhoomi, were flashing in his eyesight. While he heard someone calling his name and he looked back; with smiling face Sanjya was pacing towards him while beckoning with his hand to him to stop. On nearing, he surprisingly asked Badal whether he had escaped from the prison, but when Badal happily told him that the police released him as they found him innocent, he generously declared,

'Great! I am happy. Badal, we shall celebrate your release. You can have as much wine as you want.' 'See, just now I have come out and so I've no money,' said Badal while reversing the empty pockets of his pants. On this, Sanjya laughed triumphantly and said, 'Be worriless, that's my concern!' Listening to him Badal murmured to himself, 'Haa...! Who barely feeds himself on begged wine is offering me alms to my wish!' He smiled and asked Sanjya, 'Where to drink?' 'At my hom..' 'Let's go,' said Badal eagerly before he could finish his words. 'No, not now.' 'Not now, then when?' 'In the midnight, when everyone is asleep,' said Sanjya craftily. Badal muffled his laughter and asked, 'Have you found out a secret well of wine?' 'You can say so,' replied Sanjya promptly and left insisting on him to come to his home on the given time.

Badal sighed while running his hand on his complaining empty stomach and said, 'Great God has released me from the prison, but when will he release me from the slavery of this wine?' At that time a piercing scream accompanied with a mournful cries ran into his ears and he, being bewildered and confused, turned back to see what had happened and then smiled saying, 'Good God good! Today's daaru, fixed. My trade-goods is going to Smashan. Badal is back to work!' He joyfully shook his head and walked towards his destination dragging his wounded bare foot.